THE REAL THING

By the Author

A Chapter on Love

The Real Thing

THE REAL THING

by
Laney Webber

2020

THE REAL THING

ISBN 13: 978-1-63555-478-6

THIS TRADE PAPERBACK ORIGINAL IS PUBLISHED BY
BOLD STROKES BOOKS, INC.
P.O. BOX 249
VALLEY FALLS, NY 12185

FIRST EDITION: APRIL 2020

CREDITS
EDITOR: RUTH STERNGLANTZ
PRODUCTION DESIGN: STACIA SEAMAN
COVER DESIGN BY MELODY POND

Acknowledgments

I'm very grateful to have many people to thank. Thank you to everyone at Bold Strokes Books. I'm so happy my stories have found a home with such a great publishing house. Many thanks to my editor, Ruth Sternglantz, for her expertise, encouragement, and magical brainstorming skills. This book shines so much brighter because of you.

Thanks also to my former massage therapists for teaching me the difference between a good massage and a great massage. Thanks to the Upper Valley Vixens Roller Derby team for inspiration and fun. A big thank you to the actor Haviland Stillwell for her patience answering my many questions about acting and actors.

Thanks to my new Vermont writer friends Leslie Anne Bryce and Eileen Charbonneau for your support. My family and friends and my library colleagues have cheered me on and celebrated each new writerly milestone with me—thank you.

To the woman who has chosen to walk this part of my life journey with me: Every love story I write is a tiny reflection of the best love story of all, ours.

To Louie, always

CHAPTER ONE

The old village of Proctor's Falls had a town green with a few wooden benches and a white gazebo at one end where the community band played monthly concerts during the summer. This July afternoon, it also had Buster's golden mix running around with something in his mouth.

Allie McDonald saw the dog as she pulled around the green and into a parking space at the Harvest Hill Wellness Center. She took the lead she always kept in the car and a dog cookie from the bag in the glove box and went after Buster's dog.

"Hey, Elvis, whatcha got there?" She held the lead behind her back and the cookie out in front of her. "Did you get loose again?"

The dog had his front paws and muzzle down, rear end up high, while he worried what looked like an old blue knit hat. He looked at the cookie in Allie's hand, gave the hat an absentminded last chew, and jumped up and almost on top of Allie. She popped the cookie in his mouth, found the metal loop on his collar, and snapped the lead on. Elvis finished the cookie in one crunch and a swallow. He tried to go back after the hat, realized he was hitched, and promptly sat down. Allie gave a little tug on the lead.

"C'mon Elvis. Let's go."

The dog didn't move. Allie saw Robin, one of the other massage therapists at the Wellness Center, getting out of her car, and sketched a wave in Robin's direction.

"Hey, Allie, are you taking care of Buster's dog?"

"No," she yelled across the green. "He was loose, and I'm trying to bring him back to Buster's, but he won't move." She tried to walk nonchalantly toward Robin, but Elvis was doing a great imitation of a dog statue.

"I'll call Buster." Robin went inside the Wellness Center.

"At least you picked a spot in the shade." She patted the dog on the back of his neck and rubbed behind his ears.

She looked across the green at the big cream-colored Victorian house with the words *Harvest Hill Wellness Center* hanging from the black lamppost near the walk. If the trees behind it weren't so dense, she knew she'd be able to see the top of Harvest Hill, and Durkee Mountain beyond that.

She was so proud of her name on that sign—*Allison McDonald, LMT*. She'd been working as a massage therapist for about a year down in Massachusetts when her cousin Barb called and asked if she might want to come to the farm and help her out after her hip surgery. Allie always loved visiting the farm, and Barb felt more like an aunt than a cousin. She'd always invited Allie to the farm in the summer when she was younger.

Now two of her big life dreams had come true—owning her own business and living in Vermont. Her number three dream was to build a life with someone and live in this town.

She was learning that rural life for a single lesbian was very different than her former life in Massachusetts, where there was something to do every weekend. It seemed like all the social life was a couple of hours north in the more populated areas of Montpelier and Burlington. She'd gone out on a date or two with women who were friends of friends of Barb's, but neither of those went past the first date. There was no chemistry, and she wanted chemistry.

But there was hope for dream number three now that she knew Lauren. They both loved living in the country. They both were ready for a serious relationship. She was a beautiful person, and Allie couldn't wait to actually meet her in person.

Robin reappeared on the porch. She cupped her hands around her mouth and yelled.

"Buster should be here any minute!"

Allie gave her a thumbs-up and tried to get Elvis to move. Again. Nothing moved except his lip. When Elvis got excited or upset or nervous, the right side of his lip curled up. Buster said he'd done it ever since he was a puppy, and that's how he got his name. She tucked her hand in her armpit to feel if she was sweating through her shirt. She was. Great, and she had a whole afternoon of clients. Nobody liked a stinky massage therapist. She always kept an emergency outfit in her office, and she tried to remember if she'd already used it.

Buster owned the general store, over in the new village of Proctor's Falls about two miles from the green. Ha, she was finally thinking like she belonged here. Locals referred to the distinct two areas of town as the new village and the old village. It had confused Allie when she was younger, but she was used to it now after living here for over a year. She thought she saw Buster's truck coming over the hill and down Main Street. Elvis wagged his tail and looked up the road. She tried to hold the lead as Elvis bounded across the green to get to his owner but gave up and dropped it.

"Thanks, Allie." Buster held the truck door open, and the dog took a practiced leap inside. "Stop by the store and I'll give you a thank you. He must have followed some kids out of the store again. Darn friendly cuss he is." Buster joined Elvis in the truck.

"No problem, Buster." She waved at Buster and Elvis as they drove past her.

She stopped into The Country Bean for an iced coffee like she did every workday, but there was a long line. No one seemed concerned by this, probably because this was the only place to get coffee in the villages, except for the breakfast-lunch place next to Buster's in the new village, which was always crowded.

"Hey, Allie."

A tall man in an orange *Gotta Fish* T-shirt crooked his head and tipped his chin in her direction. She was pretty sure he was a one-time client. She had quite a few of those. Friends and relatives would give someone a gift certificate, and they'd come in for a massage once but usually didn't come back. They'd say they couldn't afford it, or it wasn't for them, and that never hurt her feelings. She knew how hard most people in and around this town worked just to keep even.

Okay. She admitted it. All this random thinking was about trying to distract herself from thinking about her phone date with Lauren tonight. She wished they had internet at the farm so they could video chat there. Other people who lived on the hill had satellite internet, but even if Barb wanted internet—and she didn't—they couldn't get a good enough signal because of the tall pines behind the house. Her friends from Massachusetts couldn't believe there were still places in Vermont without cell or internet service.

But Lauren didn't seem to mind that all she had at home was the phone and couldn't text or email unless she went into Proctor's Falls. She liked that about Lauren. She was so easygoing. Allie got her coffee, found her extra set of clothes in her office, and checked her online calendar for the day. The rest of the day went exactly as she planned, and she was able to leave the Wellness Center at six p.m.

"You're home early," Barb said. "Are you going to have time to eat dinner before she calls tonight?" Barb stopped stirring a pot on the stove and pointed the wooden spoon at her.

"I've told you Lauren has a quirky schedule, and she takes care of her mother sometimes. I don't want to miss her call because she usually can't call back." Allie dropped her bag onto the deacon's bench by the door. "It smells really good. Pasta?"

"It will be a cold pasta salad, which I'll need because I'm melting like a stick of butter. All I'm saying is she should respect your time like you respect hers. She always seems to call during supper or late at night." Barb turned off the burner and drained the pasta in the kitchen sink.

The house phone rang, and Allie picked it up before the second ring was finished.

"Hi, this is Allie." She nodded at Barb. "Hey to you too. How was your day?"

Allie pointed to the pasta and mouthed, *Save me some*, then brought the phone upstairs to her room. She would never tell Barb, but since Lauren started calling, she'd gotten into the habit of stopping on her way home for a snack, just in case Lauren called during dinner. Plus, she was usually so excited to talk to her by the end of the day she didn't have much of an appetite.

"Sorry I'm calling early, but I have to go over to my mom's later and check on her."

Allie propped her pillows against the headboard and climbed onto her bed.

"How's your mom doing?" It was so good to hear Lauren's

voice. She took the copy of Lauren's profile picture off her end table and put it on the bed beside. She looked at it while she talked.

"Some days are good and some not so good, but my brother and I have things under control. But I want to hear about your day, my sweet Allie."

"It started out with a dog on the loose, and then I had clients this afternoon. I missed you." Allie put her fingertips on the photo of Lauren. She was so happy they'd found each other online, but she wanted to touch her. She wanted to hold hands with her and walk around Proctor's Falls and show her all the things she loved about it.

"I missed you too. We'll see each other tomorrow on our video chat. I can't wait. I know it's been tough with all the stuff I've had to do with my mom lately. I'm sorry things don't always go according to schedule. Meeting you was one of the best things that's ever happened to me, and then the rest of my life goes to shit. That's not fair, is it?"

Allie smoothed the blanket next to her as she spoke, as though she was touching Lauren and trying to soothe her.

"It's okay, I totally understand. Family comes first for both of us. It's one of the many things I like about you. Sometimes life doesn't seem fair, but you're able to share what you're going through with me, and that's a good thing. Maybe we met so you wouldn't have to go through all this alone." Allie realized she was patting the blanket and stopped and put her hand in her lap. She rolled her eyes at herself. No wonder she had a passion for her work as a massage therapist. She made sense of the world and her feelings through touch or some other type of physical action.

"Maybe you're right. Did you have enough time for dinner?"

"I'm all set." It was only a partial lie. She didn't feel hungry right now and she was afraid if she said no, Lauren would end the phone call, and she'd have to wait until tomorrow to connect with her again.

"I had an idea," Lauren said.

"Okay..." Allie pushed the pillows behind her and sat up.

"You know how we've been talking sexy at the end of our calls? I thought tonight maybe we could go for a twofer. I love getting you all revved up. I love the way your breathing changes and how your voice changes."

"I know you do, but we never have a chance for me to do the same to you. I'm not sure I know how—I've never done this before, but I'd like to." Allie got up off the bed and took off her bra while they talked. Then she changed into a pair of pajama shorts and got back into bed.

"Let's do some sexy talk, then some regular talk. That will get me so horny that when we end the call like we usually do, I'll probably explode."

Allie's heart picked up speed thinking of Lauren getting as excited as she did. She wished she could see her and touch her. It was hot talking like this, but it was frustrating too. She always felt like she was on the edge, even after she came. Would it be the same in person? She thought maybe it would be more intense but maybe their connection was only intense because they weren't together in person. Ugh. Barb was right. Sometimes she thought about things too much.

"That sounds great."

"You're already thinking about it, aren't you? I can hear it in your voice."

"Yes." Allie shifted the phone into her left hand so her right hand would be free. She bent her knees and ran her fingertips down the inside of her right thigh, then ran them along the edge of her shorts.

"I'm going to tell you what to do, okay?" Lauren said.

"Okay." She knew she was already wet.

"Take off your bottoms, and tell me when they're off."

Allie put the phone down and took off her shorts. She pulled the cotton spread and blanket down to the foot of the bed. Then she pulled the sheet down and rearranged the pillows and got back into bed. She picked up the phone.

"All set. Bottoms off." She laughed.

"You're so cute. Don't do anything unless I tell you to do it."

Allie's breathing accelerated. "Okay, I won't do anything unless you tell me."

"I'm already hot, picturing you on your bed without any bottoms. Bend your knees and spread your legs for me, Allie. I wish I could kiss you. I can't wait to kiss you, Allie."

"Can I ask you to do something?" She knew Lauren liked to be in charge of this part of the phone call, but she wanted some control too.

"You know how I like this. And you like it too. I can tell."

"I don't want to tell you what to do. I only want you to tell me what you're feeling when I do things." She wanted to know what was going on with Lauren.

"Oh...I get it. Will that make you wetter, Allie?"

"Yes." The thought of Lauren getting as worked up as she did made her even more aroused.

"You want to touch yourself, don't you, because you're already very wet, aren't you?"

"Yes. Please." Her words came out in breathy sighs.

"Put a finger inside yourself and tell me how wet you are."

Allie slid her hand down her stomach and put one finger inside of herself. She groaned and her hips arched. The first time she and Lauren talked like this, she was so self-conscious and thought Barb could hear her, even though she was very quiet. But Barb hadn't given any indication that she knew what they did on the phone. And it helped that she knew Barb watched her TV shows after supper each night. But even so, she still tried to be quiet.

"Oh, baby, you've got me squirming in my seat. You are so beautiful, Allie, and so hot. Move your finger in and out. Are you very wet?"

"I'm...so...wet." Allie put the phone down and pulled the pillows out from behind her so she could lie flat on the bed. It had been so long since anyone had touched her like this. She wanted Lauren inside her. She tried to imagine these were Lauren's fingers.

"I'm going to touch myself now." Lauren murmured something Allie couldn't understand. "Damn, what you do to me. Now pull your finger out and start rubbing you-know-where." Lauren chuckled. "You know where I mean, honey. And rub it faster and faster. Let me hear you, honey. Let me hear you."

Allie heard Lauren breathing heavily on the phone and tried to picture what Lauren was doing to herself. She could feel her body almost ready to orgasm. She could hardly get any words out.

"I'm going to...going to..." She turned her head and buried her face into the pillow while she clenched her teeth, and the waves of her orgasm rolled through her body. She tried not to cry out, and the pillow absorbed the little sounds that escaped. She kept the phone next to her mouth, though, because Lauren wanted to hear everything.

"Oh, honey. You're so gorgeous. I feel so close to you right now."

She heard Lauren's words as she felt the muscles in her body relax.

"I feel so close to you too." She put the pillow behind her head again and pulled the sheet up over her legs. She felt a little chilly even though her room was still very warm from the hot July day. "Isn't it funny that we can feel so close even though we haven't met in person?"

She had missed having someone to confide in. She hadn't had a girlfriend in a few years before moving to the farm, because she couldn't sustain a relationship and take care of her parents. She loved that Lauren had the same sense of loyalty and responsibility to her mother that she'd had to her own parents. It was one more thing they had in common. Even though Lauren was in Maine, she knew they'd be able to work out the distance between them once things calmed down.

"Why don't you get yourself something to drink and I'll hang on," Lauren said. "I know your throat gets all dry after all that heavy breathing."

"You pick up on everything. I'll be right back."

Allie put on her shorts, went downstairs, and filled a water bottle. She heard the living room TV on her way which made her feel so much better about what just happened in her bedroom.

She settled back on her bed. "I'm back."

"I'm so happy right now."

"Me too."

"Tell me more about when you first moved to Vermont. I want to hear you tell me a story while your voice is all deep and sexy from phone sex."

"I don't think my voice is sexy at all." No one ever thought her voice was sexy—before, during, or after sex. Or if they did, no one ever told her. When Lauren complimented her, she felt so happy inside, and she loved to compliment Lauren. It seemed to catch Lauren off guard in some way.

"I'll tell you the story, but I want to tell you how wonderful you are. You always remember everything we talk about, even the tiniest details. You're interested in my life and my work.

I'm so happy I let my friend convince me to try that dating app thing. And thanks for putting up with the no internet at home thing. I know it must be frustrating for you. It is for me."

"It's not that frustrating. And your voice is sexy as hell right now. We both love living in the sticks. Goes with the territory. Now tell me your story and get me all hot and bothered."

CHAPTER TWO

Allie put her coffee and laptop on the table in the small conference room at the Stipple Library and closed the door. The library not only had an internet connection but also air conditioning, another amenity her cousin Barbara's farm lacked.

She turned on the laptop and tapped her fingers on the tabletop in anticipation. She was finally going to have a face-to-face meeting with Lauren. It was almost two months since Lauren shot a Cupid's Arrow at Allie's profile on Rural Rainbow Matches, and Allie swiped an arrow right back. At first, they sent messages on the app, but Allie needed to be in town to do that, so she gave Lauren her home phone number at Barb's. They talked almost every night. Maybe it was because they were on the phone that Allie found herself revealing her hopes and dreams and fantasies more than she usually would.

Her stomach fluttered as she thought about their last phone call. The past couple of weeks their phone calls had moved into steamier and steamier territory. It had taken her a long time to get settled and go to sleep last night. She had to remember she was in a public place today.

The video chat site had finally loaded. She was a few minutes late for their appointment, but there was no message from Lauren. Allie looked out the glass door of the conference room at Bethany, Stipple Library's one and only librarian, who was shelving books. When she first came to stay at her cousin's farm, she'd visited the library every day for DVDs and to chat up the most beautiful woman in Proctor's Falls. Bethany was always professional, and it took Allie almost a week to find out Bethany was very happily married and very happily straight, as were most of the women she met in this part of Vermont.

Allie tapped the space bar to wake up the computer. Nothing. This was the second time Lauren hadn't shown up for their video chat. She took her cellphone out of her backpack and called Lauren. The phone went to voice mail. She stifled the bubble of anger that tightened her chest and tried to sound open and cheerful as she left a message.

"Hey, Lauren, it's me, Allie. I'm at the library. Weren't we going to video chat today? I hope I don't have the date wrong and I hope everything is okay. I'll be home tonight for our regular phone call." She hesitated. "I miss your voice."

Allie returned her phone to the backpack, unplugged her laptop, and gathered up her things. Her cell phone rang. She wrestled with her backpack—it must be Lauren, and she didn't want to miss the call. She was feeling ticked off that Lauren missed their video chat again. She knew things were unsettled with Lauren's mother, but to not even leave a message, that was plain rude.

"Hello, Lauren?"

"Naw, it's just me," Barb said. "Can you pick me up some stuff from Buster's?"

"Sure. What can I get you?" She was definitely going to let Lauren know that she was kind of pissed that they did all this arranging to video chat, and then Lauren didn't show. But she tried to cover the disappointment she felt. Her cousin wasn't a big fan of her online relationship.

"Did Miss Sweet Cheeks stand you up again? You wouldn't stand for that if you were on a real date. You know that, don't you?"

"She has a lot going on. Her mother isn't well. She has to travel to get a signal too, and she has crazy hours at her job." Allie was getting tired of defending Lauren to her cousin and to herself. But they had so much in common, and she couldn't remember the last time she'd been so turned on by anyone. Thinking about Lauren's voice while she was getting her laptop ready had made her very aware of several areas of her body. Which was part of why she was annoyed now.

"I'm just saying maybe if this *is* dating, you should start treating your meetings like you would real dates." Okay, maybe Barb had a point. "She's stood you up on the phone, on the computer. I know she's way up in the boonies in Maine, but you'd think she'd want to meet in person. Oh, and half a gallon of milk, some of Buster's bison, maybe ground for burgers, and see if there's any of the Two Guys doughnuts left."

"You know the Two Guys bakery stuff sells out by nine. And she does want to meet me in person. We're set to meet in two weeks," Allie lied.

"Good, you shouldn't let this keep stretching out. Are you going to the Center or coming straight home?"

"I don't have any appointments tonight, so I'll be home in a few." She was so glad she didn't live alone.

"Don't forget my burger," Barbara said.

"Not to worry, cuz."

❖

Barb scooped the burgers from the grill and called to Allie. She sat on the back deck of the log home with Barb and a pitcher of iced coffee. The late day sun filtered through the tall white pines that towered above the house on the rise, casting cool shadows on their table and chairs.

"You really like this internet person?" Barbara asked. She pointed to the cordless phone in Allie's lap as she stretched her legs and hooked her boots on the deck rail.

"I think I might be falling in love with her. She's all I think about. We have so much in common. We want the same things, and I'm super attracted to her. Like, over the top attracted to her."

Her cousin sighed and looked out toward the barn.

"Are you worried about me meeting someone and running away to get married or something?" Allie said. She turned in her chair to face Barb. Allie was thirty years younger than Barbara's sixty-three years, but Barbara was so fit from physical work they appeared closer in age to anyone who knew them.

"I just don't know why you're in such a rush to pair up with someone." Barbara turned to look at her fondly. "It's your good care that got me back on my feet so soon. You can stay here as long as you want. You know that, don't you?"

The phone in Allie's lap rang.

"Two's company and all that." Barbara removed her feet from the rail and her boots landed hard on the deck. She piled dishes and condiments onto a large tray.

"Hi, you." Allie took her iced coffee and walked into the house and upstairs to her room. "Everything okay? I waited at the library for a while." She shut the door to her room and sat on the bed.

"Oh, Allie, I'm so sorry, honey. It's my mother again. I was driving to her house and couldn't call you."

"Is she okay?" Part of her was concerned about Lauren's

mother, but another part was angry at Lauren's continual excuses.

"I'm there now. She had another dizzy spell and wanted me to come over and spend the night. I got caught up with things, but she's settled in now, and I'm all yours, sweet Allie."

Allie kicked off her shoes and got onto her bed. "I know we've talked about this before, but I don't want only a phone relationship. I want to see you. I want to spend time with you. I know today was about your mother, but I want to make plans to meet. Not online. Face-to-face in person. You want that, don't you?" Her heart pounded as she said the words. She didn't want to push Lauren and scare her away, but she wanted to be honest about what she was looking for.

"Of course, I do. But, honey, my life is more complicated than yours right now. I'm over here in Maine, and you're over there in Vermont. I think we're getting to know each other in a deeper way, without all the distractions. If we were on a date tonight, say at a restaurant, we'd have to talk to the waitperson, then we'd be eating, there'd be other people around, maybe loud people telling bad jokes. We'd be distracted. Here, on the phone, it's just you and me. I'm focused totally on you and getting to know you. And we've been getting to know each other better the past couple of weeks, haven't we?" Lauren's voice grew husky and soft.

Allie cleared her throat and took a sip of iced coffee. "Yeah, that's not something I'm used to. I mean, I've never… until now…on the phone…talked about…" She felt warmth spreading between her thighs as she thought about their conversation last night. Each night Lauren went a little further in her phone seduction. This past week the conversations had gone beyond steamy to sizzling. Sometimes Lauren would abruptly stop and ask Allie how many massage sessions she had that day or what she ate for supper. Lauren seemed to enjoy putting Allie's body in a state of arousal and leaving her wanting. Now when she heard the tone of Lauren's voice drop on the phone, it was enough to get Allie's body charged. But she wanted answers first.

"I don't want to go there until we get this settled." Allie sat up in bed and crossed her legs.

"Okay, let's make a date to meet," Lauren said.

"Soon?" Allie looked around her room for her cell phone. "Let me get my calendar."

"You don't have to, honey. I've made you wait long enough. How about tomorrow?"

"Tomorrow? What about your mother?" It seemed odd that Lauren would leave her mother if she was sick and come all the way over to Vermont.

"I've already made arrangements with my brother to look in on her the next few days. I felt so bad about missing our video chat today. It's all set. If you can squeeze me in to your busy schedule…?"

Allie looked at her calendar full of appointments at the Wellness Center in the morning and at the Blueberry Bed and Breakfast in the afternoon. Along with her business at the Wellness Center, she saw clients at two bed and breakfasts in Mortonsville, just south of Proctor's Falls. The Vermont Cheesemakers Festival was this weekend, and all the inns around this area were full of people doing the Vermont Cheese Trail before they went to the festival. She was an independent contractor at the Wellness Center. She'd worked so hard to build this business. If she saw Lauren tomorrow, she'd be giving up a lot of business and potential new customers. Was it worth it?

Then she thought about kissing those beautiful lips and

touching the rest of the body that went with them. It was totally worth it.

"I have a few appointments tomorrow, but I can reschedule them. Do you want to meet halfway? I think Gorham, New Hampshire, is about halfway." She mentally ran through possible meeting places between here and there.

"No, honey, I'll come out to you. Where do you want to meet?"

Allie felt wary about bringing Lauren to the farm to meet her cousin on such short notice. And where would Lauren stay? She certainly wouldn't make a three-and-a-half-hour trip both ways in one day, would she?

"Are you coming out all this way just for the day?"

"Well, from our phone conversations lately, I was hoping you might extend an overnight invitation if we're as good together in person as we seem to be on the phone. And don't forget, I know how long it's been for you, Allie. But if the past few days are any sign, I think you'll be ready for me when I get there. Won't you?"

Allie's body responded to Lauren's words like they were caresses. She flushed, remembering how she'd told Lauren the truth about taking care of her parents and her nonexistent sex life for the past three years.

"I can't wait to meet you and see you in person. All the photos you sent are sort of blurry except for your Rainbow Match photo, and the video chat thing hasn't worked out like we thought it would." She'd heard stories about people who used the most flattering photos for their profile pics, and didn't look quite like the photos in real life, but she didn't care. Lauren was kind and smart and sweet and so incredibly sexy. There wouldn't be anywhere to stay near her with all the festivals going on, but she could get them a hotel room at the big tourist hotel off Interstate 91.

"Where should I meet you? I want to see where you work and your farm."

"GPS won't bring you to the farm, so why don't we meet at the library. It's the Stipple Library in Proctor's Falls. They open at ten." She started to make a list in her mind of all the rearranging of clients she would need to do in order to make this happen.

"I'll leave first thing and I'll see you at your library at ten thirty. How's that?"

"I'm so excited. I can't wait to show you everything." A brief flicker of doubt passed through her mind. What if after all this buildup, there was no physical attraction when they met? What if it was all only some fantasy phone fling?

"And I can't wait to see everything." Lauren laughed. "I hope I see it sooner rather than later, if you know what I mean."

"I love your laugh. And I meant I want you to see all of my special places. No, I meant…I didn't mean…" Everything had a sexual spin when she talked with Lauren. She thought they might have to go to the hotel first, before they did anything else.

"You're the only one who can make me laugh when I have all this other stuff going on in my life. You're so special, Allie. I've never met anyone like you. And your *special places* are at the top of my list of the things I want to see in Vermont, so get a good night's sleep tonight because you won't be sleeping tomorrow night. I guarantee that."

"Lauren, you get me all worked up, and you know what I'm trying to say." It wasn't entirely the words Lauren said, but the sound and tone of her voice when she said them. *She could read me a grocery list and I'd get wet.*

"I like it when you're all worked up."

"Stop it." This was the phone dance they did. Allie had to

be convinced to do some of the things Lauren wanted her to do over the phone. That dance got her even more excited.

"You like it too, Allie—I know you do. Are we all good now? Because if you're already worked up, let's talk about some of the things I like to talk about."

Allie sighed and relaxed back onto her bed. Tomorrow couldn't come soon enough.

CHAPTER THREE

A llie called Mary Ellen, the owner of Harvest Hill Wellness Center, and asked if she would be willing to take the B and B clients. Her other clients were easier to reschedule, and while one part of her was uncomfortable rescheduling them, another part of her was so excited at the thought of spending time with Lauren today after all these weeks of talking on the phone. She had spent this past year building her client list, and although some people didn't mind canceling their appointments, the practitioner was never supposed to get sick or need to reschedule.

The Blueberry B and B had been a big score for her when she first moved to town. Sally, the owner, built a spa room two months after Allie moved to town, and Sally and Barb were friends. Allie became their first choice massage therapist, and it helped build her client list.

"Hope everything's okay." Sally sounded concerned when Allie called her to reschedule.

"An out-of-town friend decided to drop in at the last minute, and she'll only be here one day. I'm so sorry, Sally." In a few hours Lauren would be in Vermont. Her body was picking up cues from her emotions. She brushed her hand over her right breast and thought about Lauren's hand touching her there, then stopped and tried to focus on the phone call.

"I know things come up and you've been very dependable with our guests this past year. But you said Mary Ellen can come?"

"Mary Ellen will be there." Sally sounded disappointed but not angry. Allie picked at a loose thread in the placemat and hoped she wasn't making a huge professional mistake. She was glad that she and Mary Ellen had an agreement about filling in for each other, but there was always this little piece of her that wondered if one or more of her clients might like Mary Ellen's way of massage more than hers.

"Talk to you soon, then," Sally said.

"Absolutely, and your guests can still book their own appointments at the B and B right through the Wellness Center's website."

Allie ended the call and looked at the rooster clock above the cookbook shelf in the kitchen. "Crap!" She grabbed her backpack and keys and headed to the library.

The clock on her dashboard read 10:29 as she parked her car in the library parking lot. She quickly scanned the outside of the library and didn't see anyone who looked like Lauren and didn't see any Maine license plates.

Allie had her phone in her hand as she pushed through the library doors and simultaneously logged on to the library's Wi-Fi. She scanned the lobby area for any faces that looked like Lauren.

"Hey, Bethany"—she approached the main desk—"has anyone come in looking for me? I'm supposed to meet someone at ten thirty."

"Mom…" A voice came from the staff room behind Bethany.

"Sorry, Allie." Bethany called back into the staff room, "Come out here if you want to talk with me. I'm with a patron." She looked at Allie. "My daughter decided to do her senior community service project here at the library." She lowered her voice and added, "Maybe not such a great idea—a little too much mother-daughter together time." She smiled. "No one's been looking for you. But it's just after ten thirty."

Allie logged into her account at Rainbow Matches, enlarged Lauren's profile photo, and showed her phone to Bethany.

"This is what she looks like. And she was supposed to meet me here about"—she glanced at the clock next to the main desk—"five minutes ago." She couldn't believe she'd cut things this close.

Bethany's daughter trudged out of the staff room and stood next to her mother. Her face brightened when she looked at Allie's phone.

"Hey, you know Geena?" She took her phone from her back pocket and started texting.

"No, I'm sorry. Her name is Lauren, not Geena. Have you seen her? She was supposed to meet me here." Allie turned to look out into the parking lot. She'd imagined that she'd get to the library, Lauren would already be in the parking lot, and they would move toward each other and hug, tentatively at first, but then like they'd known each other all their lives.

But Lauren wasn't here.

Okay, maybe she got lost, or maybe she chickened out and decided that she couldn't go through with meeting Allie. Allie hadn't slept much last night, imagining what seemed like hundreds of scenarios of what would happen when they finally met in person.

"Could you show me your phone again? Do you mind?" Bethany took her own phone out of her back pocket and her fingers typed wildly around the screen.

"Do you think you saw her here earlier?" asked Allie. She showed her the phone and her heart pounded. Maybe she came early and left right before Allie got there. That didn't sound plausible, even to her. She was spiraling, and she needed to slow down. There might have been construction or a detour. Lauren was probably delayed, and that's all it was.

"That's Geena." Bethany's daughter put her phone next to Allie's.

Allie felt light-headed. There were five or six photos of Lauren. Professional-looking photos. But why would there be all these other photos of Lauren on the web? She'd googled Lauren's name once when she was at the library. Nothing came up except one person in Texas and another person by that name in Washington State, and neither seemed anything like Lauren. But Lauren told her that she didn't do social media and wasn't online much at all.

"I don't understand. Who is this?"

"It's Geena. Just like I said."

"Who's Geena?" Allie couldn't wrap her head around what was happening. She rushed over to meet Lauren at the library, but there was no sign of her. She didn't know who Geena was or what Bethany's daughter was talking about.

"Geena is on that web series, *Days and Nights*. Oh my God, everyone loves her."

"I'm sorry, I don't know what you're talking about." She turned to look out into the parking lot.

"What *are* you talking about?" Bethany asked her daughter.

"Wait, let me show you. I think I've seen the same picture you have of her online." Bethany's daughter's fingers flew over her phone. She turned the phone around to show Allie. "See, same picture. That's Geena. I can't believe I know someone who knows Geena. I've got to tell Brittany that Geena is coming to our library."

"Why don't you go back in the staff room and finish taking

labels off the books on the cart in there." Bethany pointed to the staff room doorway.

"Wait. Can I see that picture on your phone again?" Allie held out her hand.

She looked at the picture. It was more than the head shot she had. It was a full-length shot of Lauren...or this Geena person? Her mind tried to piece together how Lauren could be this person in the photo standing on a red carpet with another woman.

"I think there's been some kind of mistake. I'm not sure who's in that picture, but I think I'm going to wait in the parking lot for my friend." She could feel blood pounding in her ears. She wasn't sure what was going on, but Lauren was going to have to explain some things when she got to town. As the thought went through her mind, Allie knew Lauren wasn't coming to see her.

"If I see her, I'll let you know," Bethany said to Allie's back as she left the library.

Allie sat in her car in the library parking lot. She stared straight ahead but wasn't seeing anything except those images of Lauren or Geena or whoever that woman was. Why would Lauren use a picture of someone else for her profile? Maybe she didn't think she was attractive enough? All the same, they'd been talking for a few weeks, and Lauren should have said something by now. They were close, weren't they? She started the car and turned on the air conditioner.

The Wi-Fi signal was weak in the parking lot, but she had cell service. She texted Lauren and asked her where she was. She called her cell phone and left a message asking Lauren to call her right away. She looked through the leaves of the tree to the road, willing a car with Lauren in it to come down the library driveway and pull in next to hers. She didn't want this to be true. She didn't want her cousin to be right.

She wasn't stupid. She'd had some questions about Lauren that Lauren never answered, but there was so much going on in Lauren's life, she'd given her a pass for a few things. Now that she thought about it, she'd given her a pass for a lot of things. Her hands trembled as she picked up her phone again to check for messages. No messages.

How could she be so gullible? She looked up and saw Bethany in the rearview mirror and put down her window.

"Hey, Allie, is everything okay? I saw that you were still here, and I wanted to make sure you're okay. You seemed pretty upset."

"I'm okay. This is embarrassing. I met someone online, and I was supposed to meet her here today. And I'm not sure what's going on, but your daughter pointed out that I may have been taken, or something…I don't know. It doesn't make sense." She felt that lump in her throat she got right before she was going to cry. She didn't want to cry.

"Is there anything I can do? Would you like some water? It's pretty hot out here."

"I'm okay. I'm going to hang out here for a while. Thanks."

"Okay, take care." Bethany headed back into the library. Allie knew in her gut that Lauren wasn't coming to Vermont today or any day. But she wanted an explanation, or something. She picked up her phone again, called Lauren's number, and left another voice message.

As she sat in the car staring at her phone, her pain started to turn outward. She was angry. What kind of person leads women on like that? How messed up is that? Allie sent one last text to Lauren.

Whoever you are, never contact me again. And I'm going to let that actress know what you're doing.

❖

"Are you sure about this?" Barbara asked Allie. "Don't you think you should wait till you're back to yourself a bit?"

"No, I think red is the perfect color for my hair. I'm done with being stupid brown haired Allie. Miss Goody Two Shoes Allie that everybody takes advantage of. I'm done with that."

"All right, listen. Let me take you into Hanover and get one of the gals at that fancy place to color your hair. Don't do the box. Just don't. You call and set up something and let me know when. My treat."

"You're probably right. But I want to get it dyed before Saturday. I'm going to take my new red hair, go up to Barre, and try out for that roller derby team. Remember that calendar announcement from the paper you put on my bureau? I emailed them, and you don't need any experience—you just have to show up. I found my skates out in a tote in the barn."

"When I saw that in the paper, I remembered how much you liked to skate when you were younger," Barb said with a nostalgic smile. "You'd even bring your skates up here and we'd all go over to the rink in Enfield and skate on Sunday afternoons. You were good. Bet you didn't think I remembered that. I didn't know roller derby was still around. No word about it that I can remember, except that thing in the paper. I used to watch it on TV with my grandfather when I was a little girl."

"I don't think it's like that anymore. I think it used to be staged, like wrestling. But now it's more athletic. I think I'll like it. I watched a couple of videos while I was at work. It might be a way to meet people. And I could burn off some of this anger about Lauren." She playfully jabbed her elbow out to the side and smiled.

"That's the first time I've seen you smile in over a week." Barbara looked at her boots. "I'm sorry that all that happened. I know I said some things about her not being a real date, but I didn't want you to get hurt. I want to say I'm sorry. You make that phone call now. I'm gonna be pulling weeds out back."

"Thanks. For everything." Allie called, and one of the stylists had an opening at eleven thirty. She grabbed her bag and cell phone and headed out the back door. "They can get me in today. But I can take care of it myself, really. Thanks for offering. I don't want you to have to hang out there."

"Well, I'll have to surprise you with something else, then," Barb said.

❖

Allie took the long way to the highway so she could stop in town at the library. She went right to the main desk and caught Bethany's eye.

"I wanted to apologize for the other day."

"That's okay. How are you?"

"I'm better. I stopped by to use the Wi-Fi for some business." Allie wanted to make sure Bethany knew she wasn't going right back online to find other so-called dates. She still felt a little embarrassed. Looking back at the past couple of months, she could see a field of red flags with Lauren's name on them that should have had her running in the opposite direction. But Lauren had sounded so sincere and they'd clicked right away. Before the other day, she hadn't even known there was a word for a person who pretended to be someone else on an online dating site: *catfished*. She thought it sounded like it felt. Lauren tried to drag her down into the mud. But she was free now, and things were going to change.

"Okay, good to see you." Bethany went back to loading books on a cart.

Allie found a quiet corner in the fiction area and logged

in to her laptop. She searched for images of *Geena*, and boom, her screen was full of Lauren look-alikes. No, she thought, Lauren was the imposter. Geena must be pretty popular—there were a ton of images online. Most looked like head shots, but when she clicked on the thumbnails, she got the full-sized image. She always had a different woman with her in all the photos. She searched for a website for the actress and found it on her first try. She'd had small parts on some TV shows and movies, but it looked like her web series was the latest and most popular. There was a Geena fan page. She read all the pages on the Geena website. She thought if she could find out more about the real woman, she might get some clues as to why Lauren did what she did.

She wondered if Lauren and Geena were anything alike. Why would Lauren pick this woman to impersonate? She was trying to make sense out of something that made no sense at all to her. Her heart hurt. She felt betrayed and a little foolish.

She found a contact page on Geena's website and put in her information, then wrote a note to Geena's publicist.

Hi there,

I wanted you to let Geena know that a woman is doing some kind of catfish scam using her photo. She did it to me on the Rural Rainbow Matches app. It took me a couple of months to figure it out, and I feel a bit foolish. The name she gave me is Lauren Metruccio. I've searched her last name online and couldn't find anything. I'm not sure if you can do anything about it, but I wanted you to know. I'm also notifying Rural Rainbow Matches. You can contact them through their app if you would like to notify them as well.

*If this is a publicist would you please forward
this information to Geena? I'd appreciate it.*
Thanks,
Allie McDonald

Next, she went to the Rural Rainbow Matches website
and told them about Lauren, then canceled her membership.
She was done being so naive. She was done being anybody's
fool. She was going to Hanover to get red hair before tryouts
with the Green Mountain Mavens of Mayhem. She was done
pursuing women. She was done with relationships.

CHAPTER FOUR

G eena sat in the bathroom stall and swiped through the messages on her phone. Campers weren't allowed to have cell phones, and the camp staff were supposed to keep theirs out of view. This was the third summer Geena had worked at Alice Jones Theater Camp for LGBT kids. She tried to keep a low profile at the camp. At first, she'd used her birth name— Virginia Harris—but some of the older kids figured out that she was Geena from *Days and Nights* the first year, so she'd been Geena from then on.

After week two or so most of the kids treated her exactly like the other adults at camp. Most of the camp staff had known her from before the web series went viral two years ago and were her summer friends, but there were always a few new faces, and some of those women found very creative ways of flirting and trying to get close to her.

But for Geena, camp was all about caring for the kids who came each summer for six weeks. She'd made herself a personal rule—no getting involved with or sleeping with anyone at camp. But truth be told, if she wasn't at camp, she'd have these women in her bed within twenty-four hours or less.

Tonight was her night off from camper duties. She washed her face, pulled the band from her ponytail, bent over and sprayed dry shampoo all over her long brown hair. She fluffed and brushed her hair while she checked her profile in the mirror.

"Not bad. The bar will be dark anyway," she said to the mirror.

A couple of texts were from women she'd hooked up with last summer. She had several bars in different towns around the camp where she went looking for fun during the camp season. But tonight, she wanted something new. She found a restaurant in a hotel in Greenfield, Massachusetts, about a half hour from camp. There should be some action at the hotel bar. And finding a room wouldn't be a problem.

She took the mini makeup kit from her back pocket and did her eyes and lips. She turned and looked over her shoulder into the mirror. Ass looked pretty good in these shorts, she thought on her way out of the bathroom.

The ride to Greenfield took a little longer than she would have liked, but she found the hotel easily, and there was parking in the back. It was a midrange chain hotel with a restaurant and bar open to the public. The door to the restaurant was in the back as well. As she walked to the bar, she looked around the room like she was meeting someone. She caught the eye of a young woman sitting with another woman at the bar. She looked away like she was still searching, then looked back at the woman and smiled, then turned and sat at the other end of the bar. *Let the games begin.*

"What can I get you?" the bartender asked.

"Do you have a nice bourbon from a local distillery?"

"Yes, we do. Millstone Brewery makes a nice one, Miller's Bourbon. Would you like to try it?"

"Sure thing."

The bartender brought her a taste of the bourbon.

She sniffed the glass, then tossed it back. "Oh, nice. Very

nice. I'll have one of those, on the rocks, please. And would you do me a favor and pour another of whatever those two lovely women at the end of the bar are drinking."

The bartender looked from Geena to the women and back to Geena again.

"Sure. Are they friends of yours?"

"Not yet." She ran a finger down the vee of her shirt.

Geena took a sip of her drink and watched the women as the bartender gave them their drinks. She did a two-finger wave and smiled at them. One of the women leaned over and said something to the other woman, then smiled a tremendous smile at Geena. Geena pointed to the seats next to her, motioning them to come to her. Sometimes she liked it when women approached her, and she made it all seem like their idea. And other times like tonight she wanted to be the pursuer. Either way she was the one in charge.

"Hi there." The shorter woman stood next to the empty stool beside Geena. Her taller friend was right behind her. "Thanks for the drinks. My friend and I had a little bet."

Geena thought the tall one looked a little shy and nervous and perfect for tonight. She had no idea if she was up for some fun with another woman, though.

"You're welcome. I saw you both when I first walked in. And it's nice to make friends with other women at the bar, don't you think? What's the bet?" She talked to both of them, but looked only at the tall woman, which seemed to make her more nervous. Was the tall one blushing? Geena loved that.

"I'm Greta, and this is Emily, and she thinks you might be someone famous, but I told her not way out here in nowheresville."

Geena looked at Emily and gave her best nonthreatening, friendly face.

"Who do you think I am?"

"Geena?" Emily bit her bottom lip after she said it.

Geena thought that was pretty hot and wondered if Greta, who didn't seem to know who she was, needed to be part of the package. She hoped not. She was pretty sure she wanted Emily all to herself.

Geena held out her hand to both women. "Emily won the bet. Hi, I'm Geena, nice to meet you." She shook Greta's hand, then shook Emily's hand and noticed her palm was sweaty.

"I can't believe you're in Greenfield. I watch *Days and Nights* all the time. I know you make the show in Boston. I keep telling Greta to watch it." Emily's words ran over each other.

"Thank you. I'm always so happy that people like the show. It's a lot of fun. I'm here because I have a summer gig in the area. But I don't know anyone here, and sometimes I get a little lonely." She looked at Emily with what she hoped was a wistful expression.

"Well, we just stopped here after work, and we're on our way home. I've got a small dog with an even smaller bladder, and he'll be looking for me. It's nice to meet you. Emily knew who you were the minute she saw you. Thanks for the drinks." Greta turned to Emily and added, "You should get her autograph or something before we leave." Greta opened her bag and searched inside.

"I'm happy to do that," Geena said, "but I'm hoping that Emily doesn't have a dog waiting for her at home." She drew her hair back with one hand, then let her hair slip from her fingers, veiling her bare shoulders. She could tell Greta wasn't interested at all, but Emily...Emily watched every move she made.

"What? Oh." Greta looked from Emily to Geena and back at Emily again.

Emily met Geena's gaze. "I don't have a dog." Her words came out fast and in one breathy exhalation.

"I can't tell you how happy that makes me. I'm happy to drive you home." She smiled and touched her fingers ever so lightly on Emily's forearm. She couldn't read Emily completely. She didn't know if she was frightened or excited or a little of both. But she did know that Emily didn't usually pick up women in hotel bars.

After Greta left, and the two appetizers and second drinks they ordered were almost gone, she wanted to take flirting with Emily a little further. Emily's cheeks were flushed, and she looked more relaxed than she had earlier in the evening.

"Well, I think you're the most beautiful actress I've ever seen. I can't even believe this is happening. I'm actually eating out with Geena."

Geena leaned toward Emily and touched her hand.

"We could eat in, you know." Geena let her eyes travel down Emily's neck and chest and lower, then back up again.

"You mean…?"

She watched Emily moisten her lips as if she was thinking about it. She could swear she could hear Emily's breathing.

"This isn't happening right now. Really? Is someone going to jump out and say I've been punked or something? Is Greta in on this? She knows what a crush I have on—"

"You're not going to be punked. It's not a joke. I think it's adorable that you have a crush on me. Isn't it funny that I just happened to come into this restaurant the same time you were here? It's like this night was meant to be. I've been thinking about what it would be like to kiss you all night."

"You have?"

"And more."

"And more?"

"Yes, much more. And isn't it a coincidence that we met at a restaurant that's also a hotel?"

Emily shifted in her seat. "You're so incredibly sexy. I can't imagine…"

"Yes, you can." Geena looked directly into Emily's eyes. Emily didn't look away.

"I can."

Emily was definitely breathing heavier now and had shifted in her seat more than once.

"I want to take all your clothes off and ravish you from top to bottom and back again. Have you imagined that?" Geena slowly ran her finger down one strap of her tank top and along the scoop front. She arched her back a little. She watched Emily's eyes follow her finger's journey.

"Yes. Yes, I have."

If she didn't get this woman into a room, it was going to be like that movie where the woman fakes the orgasm in the restaurant, but this time there wouldn't be any faking.

"Emily, let's go upstairs." She took Emily's hand.

"Yes. I can't believe this is happening. It's like a dream or something."

Geena stood up and led her out of the booth. She loved hearing how much a woman wanted her. That and the sex settled the agitation inside her. She brought her head close to Emily and whispered, "I promise it will definitely be something."

❖

Allie had her skates, her red hair, and her determination that trying out for the local roller derby team would be the start of doormat-no-more Allie. After Barb showed her the article in the local paper about the Green Mountain Mavens of Mayhem, she'd watched some videos at work and knew these were her people. And she wanted to be part of them. Maybe all those years of roller-skating when she was in school would finally be useful. She used to be so embarrassed that she was one of five kids in her class whose parents couldn't afford the skiing enrichment program at the school. She was left with the choice of bowling or roller-skating. They used the basketball court of the community building in town to skate in, with old pairs of skates that looked like they hadn't been used in years. She never would have admitted to her parents how much she loved skating and the freedom and power she felt on the skates. By the time she was in fifth grade she helped teach the younger kids when they first put on skates.

She drove to Barre and found the arena and the group of women inside.

"Put your name on the sheet that we're passing around, then lace up. Get your gear on and sit down over there." A woman with a clipboard pointed to an area near the bleachers.

Allie laced up her skates and was handed wrist, elbow, and knee pads and a helmet by a tall, athletic looking woman on skates.

"Hey, I'm Candy Crusher. You can call me Candy. I'm gonna be watching your ass today. Well, not your *ass* specifically, more like your form, if you know what I mean. Have you skated before?"

"In school, a long time ago." As she mentally did the math and the years added up, she felt a little less confident than she did in the car.

After everyone was sitting in a group, a woman named Jessica came over and talked about the history of derby, the rules, the positions, and what they'd be doing today. She said the officials and coaches wanted to watch them skate, and then they'd break them up into smaller groups and work on drills.

"Skate inside the taped area of the floor, counterclockwise, ladies."

Candy tapped Allie on the shoulder as she stood up. "Let's see how that body memory thing is. Go skate your heart out, Red."

Allie finished adjusting her knee pads with some help from Candy. She skated out onto the floor. *The track*, she reminded herself. She'd studied some derby terms so she wouldn't sound like an idiot. She was a little wobbly at first. Barb had asked Clyde the shoe repairman to fix up her old skates and make sure they were safe to use. The last time she was on skates was on a date in college. She was very aware of Candy watching her as she made her first lap around.

After a few laps they called everyone off the track and told them how often the team practiced and what kind of commitment they would have to make to join.

"There are three teams based here," Jessica said. "The Barre Bombers are seasoned, skilled skaters. The Green Mountain Mavens of Mayhem are our second-tier team, and they play exhibition matches and skate at local events to help promote roller derby. And the Rookies practice and drill here at home. The rookie players are sometimes called Fresh Meat skaters or the Fresh Meat team in other leagues, but we use the term Rookies instead. Now, those of you who still think the derby is for you, get back on the track, and you'll do some drills with some of the Mavens."

Allie learned that to skate derby you skated in a semi-squat position. After one or two turns around the track, her thighs were burning. She loved to push her body a little beyond what it thought it could do. Skating felt so good. Several women stopped skating and sat down on the floor. She kept going for a few more laps, until the skaters who were left were called off the track.

Candy skated over with a shorter skater and stopped next to Allie. "She's good, Venus," Candy said, all the while continuing to look Allie up and down.

"Yeah, she is."

"This is Venus. Don't let her size fool you. She can block anything."

"Nice to meet you." Allie wasn't sure how skaters greeted each other. Fist bump? Shake hands?

Venus did a chin bob, so she chin bobbed right back.

Candy looked at the name tag stuck to her chest. "Allie, come with me."

Allie skated behind Candy and followed her to the other end of the track where a small group of skaters and a couple of officials were talking.

"My girl goes too," Candy said.

"Where am I going?" Allie asked.

"We'd like you to skate with the second-tier team, the Green Mountain Mavens," said a short older woman with a whistle around her neck. She was one of the few people not wearing skates. "Candy says you're fast. It's obvious you're an experienced skater. Not at derby, but I think you'll catch on fast. We'll give you a try, and if it doesn't work out, you can go back to the Rookies. What do you think?"

"I think yes! I'd love to. Thank you."

"It's hard work—lots of these women will drop out after the first week of practice. I'm Amanda, one of the coaches."

Allie pointed to her name tag. "I'm Allie. I forgot how much I love to skate. I forgot how much I love the power I feel."

Candy put her hand on Allie's shoulder. "I have a few more months with the Mavens, and then I try out for the Bombers. You'll be skating with me and Venus. You'll meet some of the other Mavens during drills."

"Allie, for the first few weeks I'd like you to practice with the Rookies and the Mavens if you can. Here's a copy of the schedule." Amanda took a sheet of paper from the bottom of the pile on her clipboard and handed it to Allie.

She looked at the schedule. "I can definitely make three, but probably not all four practices. I work nights sometimes."

"If you can make it to all the Mavens practices, then it should work okay. Go ahead over with the others and do some drills. And welcome."

Allie was relieved—she thought Amanda was going to say no.

She skated with Candy onto the track.

"Next is your name. We aren't going to call you Allie. You need a derby name. If you were a Rookie, you'd have all year to pick your name, but if you're going to skate with the Mavens you'll be in uniform and you need a name. Go online and look at some derby names. Try to make yours one of a kind."

CHAPTER FIVE

Most of Geena's emails were from fans, forwarded by her publicist. She tried to answer all of them, but sometimes her schedule didn't give her the time. But she stopped scrolling through her inbox because a subject line with *catfished* and her publicist's flag caught her attention. This was not her ordinary fan email. She read the woman's email—apparently someone was using a photo of her to scam an online dating site. The woman, Allie, didn't ask her to write back or really say anything about her series or anything. But how did it take this woman a couple of months to figure it out? Allie must be pretty gullible. Photos of her were everywhere online. She typed a reply.

> *Hi Allie,*
>
>   *Thanks for writing and letting me know someone is using my photo in some dating scam. Can I ask how you found out she was using a picture of me? Thanks again for your note. I'm not sure what I can do on this end but be sure to check out my web series* Days and Nights *on the D-Verse website.*
>
>   *Geena*

She replied to a few texts and Facebook comments and was about to put her phone back in its hiding place when a reply popped up from Allie.

Hi Geena,

Thanks for your email. I'll be sure to check out your series. I live in rural Vermont, and believe it or not, up at my cousin's farm we don't have internet service. For the past two years I've gone to the local library to have internet access or sometimes stay late at work.

I do feel like I should have been smarter using a dating app, but it won't happen again. To answer your question, the librarian's daughter saw the photo I downloaded from the dating app of Lauren (you) and she knew right away (I think she is a fan from her reaction) and told me. I had never seen a picture of you (sorry). I'm not on the web much anymore.

Thanks again,
Allie

Geena looked at the time on her phone. Darn, she'd have to make this quick. Most women were too easy to seduce, but if Allie really didn't know who she was, this could be more of a challenge. Of course, she'd be up front about it. She could have a fun summer with Allie from Vermont, what was left of it. Her fingers sped over her phone screen. *Hi Allie in Vermont! I've got some errands up in the Brattleboro area on Monday—can I buy you a cup of coffee to thank you? I hope Brattleboro isn't too far to drive. I've heard a couple of people mention a coffee place called Mocha Joe's on Main Street? How's 2 pm? I'd like to thank you in person while I'm in the area. I'm at a theater camp in western MA and I only check my phone once or twice a day. Hopefully, Geena*

❖

Allie walked down Main Street in Brattleboro to Mocha Joe's café. She loved this town with its hilly streets and artsy vibe. She always said she'd get down here more often but never did. She felt a few tiny beads of sweat tickle the hairline on the back of her neck. Even thought it was only eleven in the morning, the heat rose from the sidewalk. The past few weeks, she'd watched a few episodes of *Days and Nights* and read some articles online about Geena. She liked the series, but the acting was all over the place. Geena and a couple of the other actors were very good, but the rest of the cast seemed not as professional or talented. She also found more than a little chatter online about Geena's aversion to relationships and hearts that had been broken. She'd finally given up trying to figure out the connection between Lauren and Geena, and then she received the email from Geena inviting her to Brattleboro.

She walked down the short flight of stairs and entered Mocha Joe's. It had two of her ten best smells. Coffee and pastries. The café was located below street level and was cozy and cool. She didn't feel anxious at all about meeting Geena—she was more intrigued to find out what she was like in person. The woman she'd exchanged emails with the past few days didn't sound like the actress she read about online. She knew not to believe much of what she read online, but even in interviews, Geena sounded like she was a partier and a player with a take-no-prisoners approach to dating. Allie tried to match that with the woman she'd been emailing who, yes, sounded like a flirt and a player, and who also sounded smart and kind. Maybe she was all those things. She found a table against the wall and waited.

Her gaze followed the heads that turned as a woman walked into the café, pulled her long dark hair out of a ponytail, shook it out, and returned it to its former ponytailed arrangement. Allie stood as the woman took off her sunglasses and scanned the small room. When the room scan landed on her, she felt like someone punched her in the stomach.

Her body said, *Hey, it's Lauren. Sexy Lauren, whose voice did all kinds of things to me. Who asked me to do all kinds of things to her body while she talked on the phone.* And her mind said, *Hey, it's Lauren who catfished me and used me and betrayed my trust.* Her mind and body were in a wrestling match. This wasn't Lauren. But she looked like Lauren and her body thought this was Lauren.

"Hey, Allie?" Geena wove her way around the small café tables.

"Sorry, are you Geena?" A young woman with a shaved head and several face piercings stepped in front of Geena and pulled her phone from her back pocket.

"Yes. I'm meeting a friend."

Several other people crowded around Geena, and Allie heard a small chorus of "Can I take a selfie?" "I love you in *Days and Nights*." "Can you sign my arm?" She thought it must be exhausting to be recognized by strangers everywhere you went.

"Thanks a lot. Thanks for watching the show. Thanks, everyone." Geena made her way to the table. "Sorry, that happens sometimes."

"You're very patient with them. Especially the two younger girls. Hi, I'm Allie." She stood and offered her hand. She felt her face grow warm. Standing in front of her was the woman she'd waited weeks to meet. Only it wasn't—she just looked like her. This was messing with her head. Geena shook her hand and looked into her eyes.

"I'm Geena. It's awesome to meet the woman who wants to protect me from evildoers."

They sat down.

She was trying to sort out the almost automatic flashes of anger and desire she'd felt when she saw Geena walk in to the café. Hearing her voice helped. She sounded nothing like Lauren. Everything Lauren did was a lie. The truth sat across the table from her and asked if she liked flavored coffee or the genuine article. She shifted in her seat and focused on the words being spoken, so she could answer and not look like a complete fool sitting and staring at possibly the most attractive woman she'd ever met. The photos online weren't a match for the real thing.

"I'm not into flavored coffee. But I'm not a purist either. Sometimes I put a little sprinkle of cinnamon in it." She didn't know if she should have coffee. She was a bit jangly already.

"Thanks for driving down so I could thank you in person."

"It's nice to meet you in person. Now I know there's a real person behind the photograph. When I watched you with your fans, I kept thinking you were Lauren—the woman who used your picture. My brain has your face tied to my relationship with her, or what I thought was the beginning of a relationship. But your voice saves me. It's very different from Lauren's."

"I'll have to keep talking, then. After I get some special cinnamon coffee for you, like I promised." She got up from the table and touched Allie lightly on her shoulder. "Be right back...hopefully."

❖

Several people let Geena cut in front of them, and the two teenage girls offered to buy whatever she was ordering.

"So sweet of you to offer, but I got this," she replied with her trademark sultry smile. "Please just tell your friends how much you like *Days and Nights*."

One of the girls screeched and they grabbed on to each other as they tried to take more pictures of her.

She ordered the coffees and fake studied the menu on the big chalkboard behind the counter as she formulated a plan for the rest of her summer break that included a brief affair with a very cute and very fit massage therapist from Vermont. This would be much nicer and maybe even easier than picking up women in bars and restaurants. She knew Allie was single and lonely. Probably a little cautious after that catfishing thing. She'd tell Allie all she wanted was some summer fun. She didn't want to mess with her, but she did want to have sex with her. There was something very exciting and challenging about a woman who wasn't throwing herself at her feet.

She paid for the coffees, iced for her and hot for Allie, and brought them back to the table.

"One coffee with a touch of cinnamon, for the woman who wants a little bit of spice in her life." She gave Allie her best flirty but playful look and watched Allie look away quickly. She was on target.

Allie took a sip. "Oh, this is so good. I make it this way for myself at home sometimes, but I've never thought to ask for it this way. It's nice to meet you in person, Geena. And I still feel a little dumb for not knowing who you are or how popular you are. Do you stop traffic wherever you go?"

Geena smiled. "I'm happy the series is successful, but the big success is around here in New England because we shoot in Boston, so we have a lot of college kids as fans. I chose this life, and I like the attention too—I admit that. When I don't want to be recognized, I find ways to pull that off too."

"So you wanted to be recognized today when you came here?"

"I did." She hoped someone would recognize her in the coffee shop. She'd wanted Allie to see that she was a little famous. When she was in Geena mode, lots of things were possible that weren't possible when she was Virginia Harris.

"Why?"

"Maybe I'm trying to impress you a little." She picked up her iced coffee and looked at Allie as she drank from the straw. "You seem like a nice person, and I was really touched that even though you were hurt by what that woman did, you thought about me and wanted me to know about it. That says a lot about who you are. And now that I see you, I hope you don't mind me saying you look absolutely as good on the outside. You have the most beautiful eyes." Geena put down her drink and touched the corner of her own right eye. "They sparkle like there's an awful lot going on back there that the world doesn't see." She watched color creep up Allie's neck, and she slowly pulled her hair out of her ponytail, shook her head, and let her hair drape around her shoulders. She'd be warm with her hair down, but it was worth it to see that look in Allie's eyes. She thought her hair was her best feature. This was going to be fun.

"Oh, thanks...I guess." Allie touched her neck with the back of her hand. "You're probably seeing all the things I have to do later today and this week swirling around back there. I have so much going on with my business and helping my cousin on the farm. And ever since this online dating disaster, I've been trying out some new things. I'm determined not to be a doormat or quite so gullible." Allie sat back in her chair and placed both hands on the table. "I'm taking charge of my personal life, like I took charge of my professional life when I came to Vermont."

"Good for you. But I know from experience that scammers can be pretty persuasive, especially if you're in a vulnerable place. And of course, you were if you were looking to date someone." She dragged her fingers through her hair and leaned forward. "How are you doing? If you don't want to talk about it, that's okay—we just met." She didn't really care about this lowlife who scammed other women, but she was the one thing she and Allie had in common, so she figured it was a solid first move.

Allie signed. "It feels like you're part of it all, in a way. I was so angry and hurt at first, but things have been getting better. But to be honest, looking at you brings it all back, even though I know you're not her."

The way Allie looked at her caught her off guard. She looked and sounded so sincere and honest. This wasn't the direction she wanted their conversation to go.

"Tell me more about your business. I'd really like to know." She picked up her iced coffee and leaned back.

"I'd always wanted to run my own wellness business, and after my parents' house finally sold a little over a year ago, I had the money to do it. I'd been working in a large real estate office and doing massage on the side for a few years. What about you? Have you always acted?"

"I started acting in high school. It was a place I felt I fit in. It was a good fit for me then and an even better fit now. The theater camp where I work in the summer is really great. I love working with the kids. I see a lot of kids who—" Geena stopped herself. What the hell was she doing? She just met this woman, and she was giving her way too much personal info.

But Allie was so warm and inviting that Geena felt her public persona melt a little. Time to regroup, she thought.

❖

Allie waited for Geena to finish her sentence. She hoped Geena didn't notice how flustered she was. There had been quite a few nights she'd looked at the image of that face sitting across from her right now and imagined what would happen when she and Lauren finally met. Especially after all their steamy phone calls. Thinking about that caused her heart to quicken. This wasn't Lauren, and Lauren was an asshole who used people, she reminded herself.

Geena continued, "Sorry, I'm talking too much about myself. You must have really strong hands, giving people massages all day."

Allie couldn't tell if the abrupt change in subject was Geena flirting with her. Or was it her own confusion around the fake Lauren and the real Geena? She flipped her hands over and looked at them.

"Your hands do get strong after a while. When I first started, my arms and hands would ache if I gave too many massages in one day. I had to learn to pace myself."

"They're nice hands." Geena smiled.

"Thanks." She thought that definitely sounded like flirting.

"I bet they're very dexterous."

"They have their moments." She smiled back at Geena. She didn't have as much practice at flirting as Geena certainly did, but when a gorgeous woman drove up from Massachusetts to thank her, and bought her coffee complete with a sprinkle of cinnamon, then started to flirt with her, what's the harm? Her bruised ego liked that. But on the other hand, from what she'd read online, this woman had quite the reputation for serial dating, she lived down in the city, and she seemed to be a little…superficial. But they'd barely met. She shouldn't judge Geena so harshly.

"And if you don't mind me asking, where do those lovely hands have their moments? Is there any nightlife up in the sticks of Vermont? There isn't much in Western Mass near the theater camp, and believe me, I've looked." Geena ran her fingers along the edge of her tank top strap, adjusting it a bit while leaning forward, giving Allie a view of her cleavage.

Allie couldn't take her eyes off Geena's fingers stroking her shoulder straps and the way the fabric of her top moved over her breasts.

"No, there's no nightlife." She took a sip of her now cold coffee and swallowed hard. "That's why I submitted myself to the ugly world of dating apps."

"And you lost." Geena pouted.

"I did, and when you look at me like that…are you flirting with me?"

"Yes, I am. Is it working? I can be very charming, especially around women who are as adorable as you."

Allie smiled into her coffee cup and looked up at Geena.

"You are very charming, yes."

"It's working?"

Allie nodded. She could understand why some women would follow Geena anywhere. She had an almost hypnotic allure underneath a flirty, playful exterior.

"Then will you see me again? We could have so much fun. You need cheering up after what that awful person did to you online, and I need some adult time away from the kids. Let me take you dinner or something."

"A date?" Her stomach dropped. She didn't think she

wanted to date anyone right now, but especially not the person who looked exactly like the woman who betrayed her. But the woman sitting across from her was so nice and charming and almost irresistible. Still, dating implied you were on your way to a relationship, and she didn't want to travel that road again anytime soon.

Geena persisted and said, "We each get one day a week off. My day is Mondays. Are you free next Monday?"

"I'm sorry, I'm still in recovery mode from this thing, and I don't want to date anyone right now." She felt slightly ridiculous saying that. She should say yes. Not every date had to turn into a relationship. It could be nice to go out and do something with a woman who liked to flirt. Some attention from a beautiful woman wasn't a bad thing. She kept telling herself she wanted to meet more women. Barb always said she didn't have any fun in her life besides skating, and she was right.

Her face must have given away her internal monologue because Geena replied, "I'm not talking about dating. Dating doesn't work for me. I'm all about having a good time, having fun. I don't know you, but anyone who likes cinnamon in their coffee and would take the time to tell me that someone is using my photos for nefarious schemes—even though she has been hurt by one of the schemes—seems pretty extraordinary." Geena put down her iced coffee and smiled at Allie. "I like you, and I think we could have fun together. Maybe we could go to a summer concert or a play or something like that. Get out and get away from work. What do you think? We could talk some more about your lovely dexterous hands, or something else." Geena clasped both hands on the table like a good student and looked straight into Allie's eyes.

"How can I say no?" She smiled. Somehow this woman

made her forget there were other people in the room. "I'll check and see what's going on in this area next Monday."

"Let's do it right now." Geena took out her phone and started typing. "Hey, there's a Bluegrass Jam at a brewery, what do you think? Oh, wait, it's at eight o'clock—I'd get back too late."

Too late for what? Allie thought. She raised her eyebrows.

Geena noticed. "I have a curfew at camp six nights out of seven. After ten o'clock I turn into a pumpkin. Wait, I found something. There's a circus school near here."

"A circus school? Oh, I've heard about it, but I've never been there. I'm not sure about a circus."

"Oh, not the circus. The trapeze! They have something called Outdoor Flight Days. Let's do it. It'll be wild." Geena put her phone down and took Allie's hands in hers. "C'mon—we got this."

"I don't know, I'm not so good with heights." She wasn't sure if the tremor in her stomach was from thinking about swinging over an open net or from the most beautiful woman she'd ever met, holding her hands and trying to convince her with her eyes. In that moment she thought Geena could ask her to do anything, and she'd say yes.

"I don't like heights much either, but I've always wanted to see what a trapeze would be like. Didn't you? When you were a kid? I'll be right there. You don't know this about me, but I'm a great cheerleader. If it really feels too much for you, that's okay. But why don't we try?"

Allie squeezed Geena's hands with hers. "Okay." She nodded. "I'll give it try." The answering smile across the table nearly knocked her over. She pictured herself on the floor like a bundle of rags, saying, *No, I'm fine. You smiled at me and blew me out of my chair, that's all. I'll be all right in a sec.*

"That's great. It'll be fun." Geena looked at her phone. "I've got to get back to camp, but let me give you my number, and here's my phone so you can put your number in."

"Sure."

"I'm sure I don't need to say this to you, but please don't give my number out to anyone," Geena said.

"No problem. That must be a pain." Allie put her phone back in her pocket and stood up. She pictured scores of jilted women passing around Geena's number on social media.

"I've had to change phone numbers three times in the past couple of years, but for the most part it was my own fault. You probably saw some stories online if you googled me."

Allie waited for her to dispute any of those stories, but she didn't.

Geena stood up and looked out the street level window. "It's probably even hotter out there than when we got here."

She gathered up her long, dark hair into the ponytail again. Allie was mesmerized. The entire action seemed to happen in slow motion. Geena turned and smiled at her. She smiled back, which seemed to have the effect of making Geena's smile even bigger and involved her eyes too.

Oh Allie, stop it. She'd promised herself after the Lauren fiasco that she wasn't going to repeat her mistakes of the past with women and dive in. She had wanted a serious relationship for so long and ended up driving each relationship so hard that even if it had a chance, she buried it by always moving too fast. She didn't want to be fooled by the fact that Geena looked exactly like Lauren. Of course, she wasn't Lauren, but she didn't know Geena at all—she only knew or thought she knew the woman behind the photograph of Geena. It felt so confusing.

But one thing she did know. The trapeze adventure felt like a date, even though they both agreed it wasn't.

❖

Geena drove back to camp mentally making an Allie seduction plan. Sure, it was easier to pick up a fan at a social event. But it was getting almost too easy. She always chose the activity, and most women were so happy they were spending time with Geena, she could choose anything. She always thought of it as an even exchange—the fan wanted to spend a night with Geena, and she wanted women around her who would compliment her, flirt with her, and who were passionate in their desire for all things Geena.

But Allie wasn't a fan. Allie's information about her came from an internet search, and she was wary about what she'd found. Geena took this into consideration, and she wanted to choose something for them to do that would have an adrenaline rush but wasn't seductive at first glance. She'd done that once or twice with a few anxious women, and it worked well. Even though Sunday night was her night off, she purposely chose Monday so she would need to get back to camp for curfew. A lot could happen between the end of their trapeze adventure and camp curfew, though, but she would make sure it didn't look like it was planned.

Planning and choreographing this day off was getting her a little excited. That was different. It had been a couple of years since the thought of sex with another woman legitimately excited her. Oh, she still got aroused *during* sex. But sex had become a means to hear those words of affirmation, that she was beautiful, sexy, pretty, hot, gorgeous, and desirable. The more a woman desired her, the more it soothed that ache that lived deep inside her that said she wasn't wanted. Until the feeling bubbled up again.

The thought of someone like Allie, who wasn't a fan and didn't hang on her every word and action, saying those words of affirmation excited her more than planning their adventure.

CHAPTER SIX

Monday was one of those rare summer days in Vermont with pure blue sky and no humidity. Allie drove south with her windows down and her dance party playlist streaming tunes to her car stereo. She was anxious about this adventure, or date, or whatever they were calling it. Geena had texted her over the weekend to confirm the time and tell her what to wear, but other than that she hadn't heard from her. She couldn't eat the breakfast Barb made for her that morning, and she wished she was one of those people who could feel excited about trying new things and not out of breath with anxiety. Singing helped her to remember to breathe deep and exhale, and that helped.

She followed the GPS directions to an old hay and feed store and pulled in to park. She thought she might be in the wrong place. Then she saw Geena walking toward her. The website said to dress in leggings or yoga pants and a snug fitting T-shirt or yoga shirt, and Geena had complied. Allie forgot to breathe. She could see all of Geena's unconventionally beautiful curves outlined in detail. That woman commanded every scene she was in, both off screen and on, she thought as she exhaled. She looked down and rubbed her palms against the front of her pants.

"Hey, Allie, here we are. It's adventure day!"

She shut the car windows and put her phone and keys in the small canvas bag she brought, then got out of the car.

"It's good to see you again. Is this the right place?"

Geena touched her shoulder. "You look amazing. I definitely picked the right adventure." She almost felt Geena's inspecting gaze. "I talked to a guy earlier—we go through the building, and there's a field out back where everything is set up."

"I'm not so sure about this adventure." She tried to ignore the fact that Geena's eyes felt like fingertips, exploring every inch of her tightly clad body. "In theory this sounds like fun, but I really don't like heights. I may have already mentioned that." She laughed weakly.

"Let's go check it out, and we don't have to go through with it if we don't want to, okay?"

"Okay." Allie opened the door and Geena followed her into the building. A man with a huge head of curly hair sat at a counter that held several clipboards, pens, a big jar of what looked like socks, and a placard with magnets that said *With the Greatest of Ease*, along with a large old cash register. Attached to the back of the register was a sign: *Sign in Here.*

"Hello and welcome!" The man stood up and his long curly hair bounced around his head. "Have you preregistered?"

"Yes, online. It should be under Geena?"

He looked at several of the clipboards on the counter.

"Here you are, Geena and Allie?"

Allie approached the counter. "Can I pay with my phone?"

"Oh, you're all set. All paid for." He tapped his pen on the clipboard.

Geena touched her arm and nodded. "It's on me."

"Thanks." Allie wished they had talked about who would

pay but figured Geena would be hungry later and she could treat then.

"You can go ahead out back and watch if you'd like and wait for your turn. Cal will be your instructor. He's just finishing up. Did you bring socks? We have some here." He tapped the container of socks with his pen.

Allie reached into her bag. "No socks."

"Looks like we need some of those." Geena pointed to the socks. "Why do we need socks, if we're only hanging in the air?"

"Some places don't require socks, but I've seen a few toes get caught in the netting when you land, twists them around and breaks 'em. Not a pretty sight. You never have to worry about that if you have the socks on. Just a precaution, but if you're going to fly with us, you need the socks." He nodded and his hair nodded in time.

"All the things I've been worrying about, and a broken toe was not one of them." Allie smiled hoping it would make her anxious insides feel better. The building smelled of old hay and dust. She rubbed her itchy nose.

Geena looked down at Allie's sandaled feet.

"I wouldn't want those beautiful toes hurt in any way." She beamed a smile at Allie. "Can you charge the same card for the socks?"

"Sure thing."

Geena took two pairs of socks out of the container. "Let's see what's happening out back." Geena took her hand and led her out the back doors and into the field.

Allie looked up at the large sling of netting with two very tall ladders at each end and several rectangular sets of poles that went up higher than the ladders. Everything was connected with some kind of rigging—cables and pulleys. She didn't think the setup looked very sturdy. Geena had let go of her hand as she stepped onto the field. She liked the way Geena's hand felt in hers.

Then the sight of the net and trapeze bar stopped her thoughts of how and when she might hold Geena's hand again.

"That looks really high," she said. She shielded her eyes from the sun as she looked up at a small platform at the top of the ladder where two people stood. She tried to imagine herself standing on the platform. Why did she always go along with things that freaked her out, just because a woman she was attracted to suggested them? On the one hand she wanted to try new things, especially things that were out of her comfort zone. On the other hand, this seemed really dangerous. Her fear of heights made it hard for her to figure out which one this was.

"Maybe if we watch them, it'll make you feel better about it." Geena looked at Allie's legs. "You look way more athletic than me, and this isn't a line—well, maybe it is—but do you work out?"

"Do you get away with using that line? Ever?"

"Maybe. I'll never tell."

"It wouldn't work with me." It felt good to be playful with Geena. It took her mind off the fear.

"Would you tell me what line might work with you?" Geena stepped closer to her.

"I'm not into lines." She smiled. "Back to your question, line, whatever it was. I do work out, sort of." She looked up at the person hanging by his knees on the trapeze as it swung high over the net and tried to tear her gaze away. She was aware of her heart beating. She looked at Geena instead. "I hike quite a bit in the summer and ski in the winter. But my new thing is roller derby."

"Roller derby? Really?" Geena had been watching the trapeze as well but shifted her gaze back to Allie.

She smiled as she thought about trying out for the Green Mountain Mavens of Mayhem. It had only been a few weeks since tryouts, and she loved everything about the derby.

"I love it. Everyone on the team is great. I've heard some stories about other teams, but the Mavens are fantastic. Have you ever been to a match?"

"No, but I would love to watch you on roller skates. From every angle."

Allie watched as Geena's eyes drew a slow line down to her feet and up again. She was so nervous about the trapeze that she wasn't sure if Geena's gaze made her feel desired or uncomfortable.

"Here's our guy," Geena said.

"Geena and Allie?" The tall slender man held out a hand. "I'm Cal. And I'm going to show you how to fly today. First, we'll get you each into a safety harness. Rebecca will get you all set, and then she'll go up and demonstrate what we're going to do up there."

"Hi! Who's going first?" A young woman came around from behind them. She held out two harnesses and demon-strated how to put them on. She checked them and gave Cal a thumbs-up.

"I think Geena's going to go first, since it was her idea." Allie pointed at Geena.

"And I think you're going to get more jacked up waiting down here and watching me. You go first. It'll be great. I had no idea how fierce you are, derby girl. You've got this." Geena looked into Allie's eyes and smiled.

Her anxiety melted away for a few moments.

Rebecca climbed the ladder up to the small platform and gave Cal another thumbs-up sign. Cal explained the commands as they all watched Rebecca swing on the trapeze. First, she held the bar with two hands and jumped off the platform and swung out. A man on the platform yelled, "Legs up!" and Rebecca brought her feet and lower legs up and over the bar. "Hands off!" and she dropped her hands and swung by her knees a few swings back and forth over the net. "Hands on!" and she grabbed the bar with her hands. "Legs down!" and she hung straight from the bar, holding on with her hands. "Hup! Drop!" and she dropped and bounced onto the net.

"Got it? C'mon, I'll meet you at the top," Cal said and started up the ladder.

❖

Geena took both of Allie's hands in hers, and for a moment it wasn't about her planned seduction. She wanted to support Allie, cheer her on, and give her whatever she needed. She leaned in so her face was inches from Allie's.

"Whatever you want to do. I'm here for you." She took a step backward and felt her ears grow warm.

"I'm gonna go for it," Allie said and put her hands on her hips and planted her feet. "I want lots of applause when I land in the net." Rebecca appeared from nowhere and hooked the safety line to the large carabiner on the front of the harness.

"You got it." Geena watched Allie climb the ladder. Her legs looked even stronger than Geena had first thought. Her mind went back and forth between how great that backside looked climbing the ladder and how much she wanted this to be a great experience for Allie.

She heard Cal's and Allie's voices but couldn't make out what they were saying. Then Allie took her stance, held the bar in both hands, and pushed off. Her heart pounded as she watched Allie go through Cal's commands while the trapeze swung back and forth. She watched her bring her legs off the bar and hang from the bar. And she was smiling! Geena started clapping as loud as she could. She heard Cal yell, "Hup! Drop!" and kept clapping as Allie fell onto the net and bounced around ungracefully. Rebecca stood by the net to help her come back to the ground. She unhooked Allie from the safety line.

Geena kept clapping. "You looked great up there. How was it?" She thought Allie looked strong and beautiful up there on the swing. And she was surprised at how much she wanted her to enjoy this day.

Allie was laughing as she walked toward her.

"You're great. You can stop clapping now." She laughed again. "It was a little scary at the top, but once you take off, it's incredible. I felt like I was ten years old, playing on the swings in my nana's backyard, only with a bigger rush. Your turn. It's incredible. Did I already say that?"

"Okay. I'm ready. Wish me luck." Geena hoped for a peck on the cheek, a hug, or at least a pat on the back but didn't get any of these.

"Good luck. Now I'll be your cheerleader." Allie pretended to shake some pom-poms.

❖

Allie's body was still buzzing from her time on the trapeze bar. For a moment on the platform she didn't think she would be able to go through with it. But right after she launched herself, she felt wonderful. She forgot about her anxiety and was totally focused on completing Cal's commands. Her only disappointment was it all happened so quickly. And suddenly she was down, and Rebecca told her how to remove the harness.

She watched Geena hang by her knees and swing over the net. She wondered if she was a dancer too, because her body moved like a dancer's. A few clouds toned down the glare as she watched Geena drop and bounce onto the net, as if she had done this a hundred times before. She jumped up and down with her invisible pom-poms.

"Whoo-hoo! You did it! Geena, Geena, Geena," she chanted.

Rebecca helped Geena down from the net and kept holding her hand. With the other hand she removed the safety line from the carabiner.

"I knew you looked familiar. I saw an interview on TV the other night, on that show. I can't remember the name. Are you that Geena?"

"Yes." Geena gave her a big Geena smile. "Thank you, lovely Rebecca, for all your help."

"Let me help you get out of that harness."

Allie swore she saw Rebecca lick her lips as she said that. She watched Rebecca take her time unbuckling and removing the harness from Geena. Geena looked over at her and winked.

"Can I get a selfie with you?" Rebecca asked.

"Sure."

Allie wondered what it must be like for Geena to be recognized and watched all the time. She seemed to like it, though. She didn't think she would like it, but then, she did like it when people cheered her and her teammates during a match and wanted her to autograph merch afterward. But that was different. No one knew who she was outside the arena.

"Nice to meet you, Rebecca—see you again sometime." Geena walked over to Allie.

"Oh, I hope so," Rebecca said, turning back toward the net, leaving them alone together.

"It was amazing," Geena gushed. "I loved it. I didn't think I was going to get my legs back down again."

"You looked like you had done it a million times before. You must be a natural."

"Really, you thought so?" Geena stopped walking and looked at her.

There it is again, Allie thought. The Geena switch turned off for a few moments, and she saw a softer more vulnerable woman in front of her. But just as quickly, Geena turned it back on again.

"You get a pretty nice view from on the ground, don't you think? I know I enjoyed my view very much."

She stepped in front of Geena and opened the door to the big building. This was Olympic-level flirting, and she didn't even know how to make the team. She waved to the man behind the counter with the big hair. She stopped to pick up a brochure and felt warm breath on her neck.

"You haven't told me if you liked watching me on the trapeze."

She turned to face Geena.

"I did." She wouldn't tell Geena that she watched her every move on the trapeze and thought about what she must be like in bed. But she tried to make it show on her face. "Very much."

She held the door open for Geena, whose ear-to-ear smile only dazzled her more.

"What would you like to do now?" Geena asked as they walked to the parking lot. A breeze drove up some dust from the blacktop.

"Why don't I drive us to get some food—I know I'm

hungry. I think my nerves burned up everything I ate today. My car is over here."

Geena grinned as they reached her Subaru. "Seriously? You drive the poster car for lesbians?"

"Yes, I do, but more than half the population of Vermont drives one, not only the lesbians. Look around the parking lot." She motioned with her hand, unlocked the car, and they both got in.

"I only counted five. You were so great on the trapeze. Once you did it, you didn't want to stop." She laughed and Allie laughed with her. "Your face is stunning." Geena reached across the car.

Allie turned her head and started the car. "It was great. Thank you for suggesting it—I never would have tried that on my own." She swore she could feel heat from Geena's body across the car. All she could think of was touching her. She felt warm and tried to make small talk to get her mind off her body's reaction to being in a small enclosed space with probably the sexiest and most beautiful woman she'd ever met. Every movement Geena made seemed to have sexual undertones. Out of the corner of her eye, she saw Geena arch and stretch her back, and Allie's breath caught.

"I think I might have been tense about the whole flying through the air thing too," Geena said, still stretching. "My back feels kind of tight."

"If there are any tennis balls at your camp, grab a couple and put them on the floor or against the wall, and move your back against them. That should help." She was thankful for something to talk about to take her mind off how close she was to Geena in the car.

"I almost forgot that's your gig. Maybe you could show me sometime?" Geena said softly as she reached over and put her hand on Allie's arm.

"We're here." She braked a little too hard as she pulled into the parking lot and she saw Geena jerk forward out of the corner of her eye. "I'm sorry. Are you okay?"

"I'm fine." She laughed. "You must be really hungry. I like hungry women." She took off her seat belt and turned toward Allie.

She would love to give Geena a massage and so much more. She really wanted to be the kind of person who could have some fun sex and not have it mean anything. But she wasn't sure. How long could you go without sex and not have your body burst into flames around a beautiful woman? She mentally shook her head to clear it.

"It's okay. I'm a little jumpy. Residual nerves maybe." She unclicked her seat belt and turned in her seat. "I want to be up-front with you. You know I was online trying to find someone because I haven't found many opportunities to meet women where I live. But it's been a really long time for me since I've dated anyone. I was taking care of my parents for a few years before they passed away and didn't have time to be in a relationship or date anyone. Then I thought I was ready, and look what happened. It still stings, getting catfished. I don't get why anyone would want to do that. Roller derby is helping, at least in terms of meeting women who live in rural New England. But I'm totally not ready for a relationship right now."

"And I'm really sorry if I overstepped," Geena said, her tone gentle. "I like you and I'd really like to spend more time with you and go on more adventures this summer. The kind of adventures that involve less clothing." She smiled. "I think we could have a fun summer if you wanted that."

"And then we'd go back to our lives in the fall, right?"

Even though the car was still running and the air conditioning was on, heat rose in her body. She'd never had a summer fling, with no other expectations.

She had never been a fling type of person. She'd had two one-night stands during the two years she took care of her father, and no dates at all since moving to Vermont over a year ago. She did have sex one night with a derby mate, who asked if she wanted a sex buddy. It was hot at first, then it got awkward, then they laughed about it, and it was…nothing else. She wasn't sure if that night took the edge off or heightened her desire to have sex with someone other than herself. But one thing she did know—her desire grew the more time she spent with Geena. Geena's lips were the lips she'd looked at every night for the past two months and fantasized about what it would be like to kiss them.

"Yeah, sure. But meanwhile, we'd have a great time—you know, live in the moment." Geena shifted in her seat, moved closer, and ran one finger down the edge of the car seat.

"You're so beautiful." Allie's throat was dry. Maybe if she was on the same page as Geena from the start, it could work. She'd been burned a couple of times, diving into what she thought was a relationship, because she wanted to be in a relationship so badly, only to find out that the other person didn't share her feelings. With Geena she'd know exactly what she was getting into.

She reached toward Geena's hand until her hand met Geena's. Her heartbeat grew louder and moved up into her ears.

"You're adorable." Geena leaned forward. "But I want this to be your idea."

Her face was inches from Geena's. She looked into her eyes. She leaned forward, and her lips met Geena's. Desire spiraled through her body. Even though she'd started the kiss, it was clear after a few seconds that she was being kissed by Geena. All she could do was surrender as her body responded. There was no Brattleboro, no parking lot, no car. There was only this kiss.

When their lips parted, Allie wanted more. No one had ever kissed her like this. Their next kiss led to a third, and then Allie took the lead and felt Geena soften beneath her lips and hands. Geena's hand moved to the small of her back and pulled her closer.

"Your hair doesn't lie—there's fire under that adorable exterior," Geena whispered in her ear.

"Maybe having a few adventures is exactly what I need." Her voice was husky, giving away how turned on she was. She looked into Geena's eyes. The combination of those blue-gray eyes and her dark brown, almost black hair was intense. She licked her lips.

"That and a few more kisses, maybe?" Geena touched the tip of her finger to Allie's lower lip. "But maybe not in the car. Where can we go to continue this adventure? If you're up for it."

Yes, she was up for it. She was ready to take her clothes off and climb in the back of the Subaru and shout, *Ready!*

But that's not what she did.

"I think we should get some food now and have more kisses later, if that's okay?" She didn't know why she was pulling back. She'd been ready to jump into bed with Lauren. But she thought she knew her. If she was going to have a fling, it would have to be on both of their terms, not only Geena's. She wasn't going to be taken advantage of again. From the slightly pouty expression on Geena's face, she wasn't used to women putting off her invitations.

"Sure, I have to get back soon anyway. Why don't we pick up something for the road?"

"Are you ending our adventure because I put the brakes on?"

"No, we've just met. You don't know me. I get that. But, Fireball, we only have the rest of the summer to play. And I'm pretty good at figuring out who wants to play with me."

Allie's heart sank. "I've been played by another woman recently, and you're right—I don't know you. I'd like to get to know you better, so I know who I'm having a summer fling with. And I want more kisses too. We can do both, can't we?" She knew it wasn't the right call as soon as the words left her mouth, and Geena appeared ready to bolt from the car.

"Um, sure." Geena glanced at the dashboard. "I really didn't realize how late it was. I'll pick up something for myself on the way back, and I'll text you. My phone is contraband at camp, but I'm on it once a day."

"Are you sure you don't have time for a quick bite? There are a couple of places right here."

Geena leaned over and gave her a quick kiss on the cheek. "Trapeze was so much fun. As were the kisses." She had her hand on the door handle as she said the words.

"I can drive you over to—"

"It's okay. The trapeze place is right around the corner. Catch you later." Geena shut the car door, knocked on the window twice, and waved good-bye.

❖

Geena found her car, stopped at a barbecue food truck on her way out of Brattleboro, and headed back to camp. She wished she had thought of a backup plan, or rather a backup woman. It had always been easy for her to choose how, when, and who she shared her bed with or not, even before her success on *Days and Nights*. She'd seen the way Allie looked at her when they first met for coffee. It was the same way some of her fans looked at her. They watched her perform, they trolled images of her online, and when they met her in person, most of them had fantasies that she was usually happy to make come true for a select few.

All she wanted was to have other women want her and want to be like her. She managed her image off-screen to match the women she often played on-screen. They all knew Geena, but none of them knew Virginia Harris, except her two older sisters, and one former girlfriend from college.

As she drove, she tried to figure out what went wrong with her plan. The adrenaline-rush adventures were great because either her date had that great endorphin flood after having done something she never did before and those happiness molecules usually traveled all over her body, or if the adventure was a bust, Geena had the opportunity to console her. Either way, a few kisses afterward always led to a bed somewhere.

Not on her adventure with Allie. Allie had sounded like she wanted to take her up on her offer of some summer fun. Then suddenly, she hit her with this get-to-know-you-better stuff. That was for relationships. Geena didn't do relationships. Next week, she'd go to the bar in Springfield. Last year she'd had a couple of uncomplicated one-nighters with a woman named Marcy who worked at a burger joint. She was a lot of fun. Marcy said she'd keep an eye out for Geena this summer. She wondered if she still had her number.

But then she touched her lips with her fingertips and thought about kissing Allie, or rather about the way Allie kissed her. And for a moment, she forgot she was Geena.

CHAPTER SEVEN

Allie went straight to the barn when she got home to find Barb. She almost stopped a half a dozen times on the way home to text Geena and apologize for being so out of practice at dating, or having a good time, or whatever they were doing.

"Hey, Barb, you in here?" She walked to end of the barn and out the back doors. She found Barb there, brushing down her horse, Canada.

"How was flyin' through the air with the movie star?"

"I'm an idiot."

"What did you do now, get engaged?"

"That's not funny." She picked up a brush and worked it down the horse's neck in short strokes. "We had a great time. Then I wrecked it when things got a little hot and heavy."

"I doubt you wrecked it. He's done on that side, you know." Barb clipped the lead on his halter and led him into the barn and his stall.

"I'll get the brush kit. She was up-front with me and told me she was only looking for some summer fun, and I thought, why not? I always do everything according to my plans for the future, why not do something without a plan?"

"Yay, you. Nice. Here take these."

Barb handed her the halter and lead, and Allie put them

and the brush kit in the tack room. Barb shut the stall door and came up behind her.

"We kissed, and then she suggested we go somewhere."

"Ooh, love the one you're with, baby."

"Have you been drinking?" Barb was usually protective of her, and now she was throwing her to the wolves, or the she-wolf anyway.

"I've watched you try to take care of your mother for years, and then after she passed, you decided, against my and your brother's better judgment, to move in with your father and take care of him during his last few months on the planet. You've always worked hard. First at school, then at your job at that real estate company. Then you came up here to take care of me after my surgery."

"I still don't think you really needed my help." She walked next to Barb on the path to the house.

"Anyway, you haven't had a whole lot of time for fun. You plan a lot, and I give you points for that. And I know you want to get married and that whole ball of wax, but for God's sakes, have some fun, Allie. Did you have fun?" Barb opened the back door and went inside the house. "There's some leftovers in the fridge."

"Yes, it was fun. It was great. We kissed, and then she wanted to take things someplace else and I froze. I don't know if I can simply have sex with someone and not know anything about them."

"Why not—have you tried it?"

"Yes. Well, no. Well, kind of. I hooked up with one of my mother's aides, but I'd had a few drinks and I was lonely and she kind of seduced me. I never saw her again—those aides from the state go from job to job. And that night I was really late getting home a couple of weeks ago? I was with someone from derby. I told her I wanted to have sex with *someone*, and she said, *Why not me?* So, we did. It was fine. It was just sex." But her body hadn't reacted to Princess from derby like it did to Geena.

"You had sex with this gal, and now this Geena wants to have sex with you and you blow her off? Doesn't make sense to me." She pulled two glass containers out of the refrigerator. "Put these in the microwave and eat. You get cranky when you're hungry."

"I didn't totally blow her off. But she practically ran from the car after I said I wanted to slow things down and get to know her." Barb shook her head and sighed. Did no one understand what she wanted? "Don't look at me like that. I only wanted to know more about her before I go flinging myself into bed with her. She won't call me. She has, like, hundreds of women who want to spend time with her. In any capacity. And I kept thinking of Lauren and what she did to me, and it's confusing because in my mind they both have the same face."

"I didn't think of that. That's gotta be weird." Barb sat down and took her boots off. She wore boots every day year-round, no matter how hot it was outside.

Allie sat down with her two containers and a fork and started to eat.

"You have no idea how weird. I have all these strong feelings when I look at her. I'm really attracted to her, and I'm pissed too, but that's not about her. But the attraction is, I think? But I don't want to jump in bed with her because I'm confusing her somehow with Lauren. That would be using her." She chewed her food and gave her cousin a questioning look.

"Whoa, that's even weirder than I thought."

"Right? How do I know it's Geena I'm attracted to and not my idea of Lauren? In my mind they both have the same face."

"But do you care if it's just sex?"

"Ugh, it's messing with my head. I can't think about it anymore tonight. I need to get ready to go into town. I have two appointments tonight over at the inn. We'll laugh about this someday, right? Isn't that what people always say? All I know is I'm not calling her. I'm not throwing myself at anyone ever again."

"You rode that horse in your twenties."

"Yes, yes, I know. I'll do these dishes when I get home, leave them for me."

"You don't have to tell me twice. I've been fixing fence all day, so I'm beat up and going to bed soon. It'll be okay." Barb stood and gave her a hug.

"Thanks. Don't wait up."

Allie drove to the Blueberry Bed and Breakfast, and her shoulders relaxed as she thought about taking care of her clients. She loved being a massage therapist. She was a natural caregiver even though she was still learning how to take care of herself as well as she cared for others. After her first doctor-ordered massage to treat the stress of caring for her parents, she took money from her savings account and registered for massage therapy training. She had jumped from job to job in her twenties, working at a dentist office, a local radio station, and a large real estate company. She thought maybe she'd wasted her time getting her BA in business. Then massage school ignited a passion she didn't know she had.

Two years ago, with both of her parents gone and their house sold, she knew two things: she wanted to start over in Vermont, and she wanted to own her own massage practice. Barb's call to come and help happened at the perfect time.

She drove around the back of the large Colonial and parked. Sally met her at the back door of the B and B.

"The room is all set for you." Sally handed her a clipboard with her standard intake forms. "They're all filled out for you. Two really nice women, here for a girls' weekend away."

"Thanks. Have a good night."

It would be nine o'clock when she finished, and on late nights, she let herself out and locked the door. Sally would already be in bed—when she had guests, she always got up super early and made homemade scones. One time, Allie was called for a morning massage appointment, and Sally gave her two maple scones on her way out. The thought of them made her mouth water, and she'd been wishing for another morning appointment ever since.

Her massage room was off the kitchen in a small ell. In the hallway to the ell sat her first appointment—Charlotte, according to the paperwork—a woman who was older than her, but younger than Barb, with a pleasant face, deep brown eyes, and short salt-and-pepper hair. Allie brought her in the room, introduced herself, asked a few questions, then stepped back in the hallway to wait until Charlotte was ready. She read through both forms again while she waited. The sound of a small bell caught her attention. She knocked lightly on the door.

"All set."

Allie went in and dimmed the lights and turned on music.

"Is music okay, Charlotte?" She liked to use the person's name several times to help her remember it. She was horrible with people's names. She once tried writing her client's name on the inside of her arm, but the massage oil smeared it and made it unreadable. Now she wrote the name in big letters on the top of the form she used and propped it somewhere in the room where she could see it.

"Please call me Charlie. Only my parents called me Charlotte. And the music is wonderful. Thanks."

"Is there anything else you'd like me to know before we start, and would you like to start face-up first or end that way?"

"It's been so long since I've had a massage—what's better?"

"A lot of my clients like me to start on their backs because that's where we carry stress, so there's usually quite a bit of work to do there, then end the massage lying on their backs where I do lighter work on your head, neck, and face. But it's totally up to you. This is your time. This is your hour. I'm here for you." Allie spoke softly. She was always able to leave the rest of her life outside the door when she was with a client.

"Oh, gosh." Charlie sniffed. "I don't want to start crying on you. I'm real stressed and Janet, my friend, you'll see her next, wanted me to get away, so she planned this weekend." She wiped the corner of her eye.

"Here's a tissue. Just so you know, lots of people cry when they get a massage. Sometimes a massage allows you to release stress or anxiety that way. It's not out of the ordinary, and I have a big box of tissues, so hold out your hand and I'll hand you a tissue, okay?"

Charlie wiped her eyes.

"Thanks. I'll be okay. I think I'll let you start on my back, so I'll need to roll over."

"Sure thing." Allie held the sheet away from Charlie while she rolled over.

As soon as Allie started the massage, Charlie started talking. She knew some people weren't comfortable being in a room with another person and not talking. And she knew some people had anxiety, and talking helped them release it before they could really relax into the massage. Charlie was that person. After she rolled back into a face-up position, Allie could tell she was finally giving in to the massage. She could feel her muscles lengthen and soften. And finally, Charlie stopped talking.

Allie finished up the massage the way she did for nearly all her clients. She gave Charlie a facial massage, massaged her scalp, then drew her fingers through Charlie's hair slowly all the way to the ends. She placed a blanket on her and used two hands to press down slowly and evenly on her left arm, then left leg, then right leg and right arm. She found this helped ground her clients.

She loved giving her clients a place to simply *be* for an hour. Every time she gave someone a massage, she was totally in the zone and focused on each moment, so it was a respite of sorts for her own anxieties too. She hadn't thought of Geena once during that whole hour.

"Okay, Charlie. Take your time getting up. I'll be right outside the door." Allie shut off the music and left the room.

A few minutes later a tousled and happy looking Charlie opened the door.

"How was your massage?" Allie asked as she stood up.

"Oh my God, that was unbelievable. I think I went to another plane or something. I was talking to you, and then I was floating someplace that wasn't quite awake and wasn't really sleep. And my shoulder blades can move again. You're a miracle worker. You have magic hands or something. Thank you so much."

"You're so welcome—we all have so much stress in our lives. I have a really great job. I don't see your friend yet, but I'm sure she'll be down soon."

"I'll go see what she's up to. I'm sorry if I talked too much. You know practically my whole life story."

"You needed to talk a bit when we started. That's okay. Have a good night." She wanted to see her next client and get home. She was very tired. The day's stress was catching up with her.

"Thanks so much. Magic hands. Thanks, Allie." Charlie reached into her back pocket and handed her a check, then patted her hair down as she walked away.

Her second client came down a few minutes later and thankfully wasn't a talker. The hour went by quickly, and the woman was up and out of the massage room about three minutes after her massage ended. She gave her cash and a healthy tip and said good night.

Allie straightened the room for whoever would use it next. Other local practitioners used the room for the B and B's advertised spa treatments; reiki, reflexology, acupuncture, and something that had to do with tuning forks and crystals. She could never remember the name of that one. As she drove home, she wondered if Geena had texted her. She pulled into the library parking lot to check her phone.

"Nothing." Even though she'd told Barb that she wouldn't hear from Geena again, part of her had hoped she would. Part of her wanted to text Geena right now and tell her that she was ready for any kind of adventure that Geena could dream up, including an adventure between her sheets.

❖

Geena tossed and turned under the scratchy camp sheets. She knew Allie was surprised at her sudden departure earlier that day. She was probably angry or hurt. She did tell her that she'd text, but she didn't know what to say. The day didn't work out like it was supposed to. She never failed once a woman showed interest in her. Once that happened, it was usually a short trip to yes on both sides. There had been a couple of women who didn't believe her when she said she wasn't into relationships. They thought they could change her. But they found out quickly that they couldn't.

She threw the sheet at the foot of the bed. She was hot. The cabin air was still and sticky. Her roommate Melissa snored lightly from the bunk above her.

Allie's kisses had wound her up, but that wasn't what was keeping her awake. It was when Allie was jumping up and down with those damn make-believe pom-poms. That broke through her Geena persona, and she felt like Virginia for a few minutes. The outside corner of her eye tickled, and she wiped the wetness that trickled down her temple. It had been so long since she had let herself really feel anything and not block it or bat it away with a joke or a manipulative look or touch.

Part of her felt that seeing Allie again would be dangerous. Anyone who could cause her to forget her armor, even for a minute, was dangerous. She'd sworn a long time ago that she would have control over how much she let anyone see of Virginia, of her real self. Geena gave her what she wanted.

But another part of her was excited by the challenge that Allie presented. She thought she could figure out a way to get past all of that getting-to-know-you stuff that Allie threw out there and find a way to make Allie say yes. If she could do that with someone who had the power to catch her off guard, that would make her feel amazing. But she didn't want to hurt Allie. She never planned to do that—planned to hurt someone—when she started something with a woman. That was troubling. She never purposely hurt women's feelings. She never lied. She told them exactly what she could and couldn't give them. But some women probably didn't believe her.

A clap of thunder sounded directly overhead, and Geena jumped.

Melissa yelped.

"Can I come down with you?" Melissa asked from directly above her. "The top bunk feels a little too close to the action."

"Sure thing, grab your pillow," Geena replied.

Melissa climbed down and stood next to the bunk beds.

A crack of lightning lit up the small cabin, and as it faded, another round of thunder rolled nearby.

"Oh, I hate thunderstorms! Every time one happens, I think I'll be brave—it's only two air masses colliding. Where are my flip-flops? Dammit, I hate being a baby."

Geena sat up in her bunk and skootched so her back was against the wall.

"C'mon"—she patted the mattress—"you're not a baby. Everyone's afraid of something."

Melissa climbed in next to her just as another crack of lightning whipped the air above the cabin. She grabbed Geena's hand.

"You're not," Melissa said.

"I'm not what?" She was still distracted by the way her night with Allie ended.

"You said everybody's afraid of something. But you're not. In the three years I've known you, I've never seen you afraid of anything."

"Lots of people get very good at hiding what they're afraid of. It's not a rats or spiders or thunderstorms kind of thing." She tried to wiggle her fingers in her tightly held hand.

Melissa let go of her hand and looked like she was waiting for her to tell her more about her fears. She looked away from Melissa. She didn't feel like talking about what scared her.

"Sorry," Melissa said. "Did I hurt your hand? I think it's almost over." Melissa leaned back against the wall of the cabin and stretched her legs out. "Tell me about your night on the town. Did you have fun with the Vermont woman? I forgot her name."

"Allie. We had fun, but then things got hot, then strange. *I* felt strange, different. Never mind. It didn't go as planned." Melissa was the only person she could talk to like this. They'd been cabinmates and had become friends before she got the job on *Days and Nights*. She was one of very few people Geena trusted.

"No sex?"

"Nope. She wasn't into it. Then I wasn't into it. It's complicated." What *did* happen between them? And why was she still thinking about Allie? This should be done. She should put a line through Allie's name and start thinking about her next day off and where she could land for a night of fun.

"Complicated sounds way more interesting than your usual encounters. Tell me more."

"She wanted to get to know me better." Geena made air quotes.

"Lots of other women have wanted to get to know you better, usually after sex, though, not before." Melissa grabbed her pillow, crawled out from the bunk, and stood up.

"It's late. I don't want to talk about it anymore," she replied, hoping to shut down this conversation. "It was just one night that didn't turn out the way I expected. That's all." She punched her pillow a few times, then plopped down on the bunk. "Good night, M."

Melissa started to climb up the ladder to the top bunk.

"I think there's more to this one than you're telling me, but good night. Thanks for the thunder rescue."

CHAPTER EIGHT

Allie was the first to arrive at the Wellness Center the next morning. She was up early, pacing and drinking coffee while Barb tried to eat breakfast. Barb finally shooed her out of the house and told her to go check her phone someplace in town, for Pete's sake. She checked it before she got out of the car at the center. She knew Geena said she would call or text her, and she'd planned to wait, but she thought she should at least thank Geena for the great adventure. And that's all she said in the text she sent. *Thanks for the trapeze adventure.*

Colleagues started pulling into the parking lot, and she got out of her car and tried to head off Bruce, who was carrying a portable massage table.

"I'll get the door," she said.

"Thanks, Allie. This thing is beastly awkward."

After Bruce made it through the doorway, he was followed by Mariah the acupuncturist, who had Elvis the dog behind her, followed by an older man carrying a flower arrangement.

"Is there an Allison who works here?"

"I'm Allison."

He pushed the vase into her hand. "Here you go. See ya." He took off down the walkway like a race walker.

"Can you watch this ding-dong dog?" Mariah asked. "I

don't have my phone and I have to call Buster. That dog's going to get hurt one of these days."

"Elvis. Sit." Allie gave the command half-heartedly, never thinking he'd obey. Elvis plopped his furry backside down, and then he landed on his side and sprawled out on the waiting room floor.

"I'm not patting your belly. I've got clients to see." She said it loud enough that anyone behind the desk could hear.

"I brought the goofball in—I'll handle him," Mariah said. "I'm taking him out back until Buster gets here. It's fenced in." Elvis followed Mariah like she was a pork chop.

It was so nice when people sent flowers, she thought as she plucked the card from the bouquet. *Thank you for the life-changing massage. Charlie.*

She put the vase on the reception desk and picked up the phone to check messages. One was for another massage therapist, and one for Mariah. She wrote them all down. The Center had a very part-time admin person who worked two days a week, and the rest of them filled in answering the phone and taking messages. Everyone here rented a space in the building and took care of their own business needs. Mary Ellen owned the building and the name and provided the part-time admin. Allie's business was thriving, and she often thought about buying the Center if Mary Ellen ever decided to sell.

She brought up her calendar on her phone and checked her schedule for the day, then holstered her phone and went down the hall to the last room on the right. As soon as she stepped into the space, she felt like she did the very first time she came to the Wellness Center after Barb shoved the address and phone number into her hand and all but pushed her out of the house. The soft green walls and diffuse natural light were a peaceful combination. All she'd done with the space was add a couple of woodsy prints on the walls, her two Himalayan salt lamps, and a silk fern in the corner. She loved her space, and her clients let her know they did too. She saw her two appointments, then took a walk to the bench in front of the post office and ate her lunch. She never ate in her massage space. She didn't want to assault her clients' senses with the smell of her leftovers, or any food for that matter.

When she came back from lunch, Charlie was in the waiting room.

"Thank you for the flowers." Allie pointed to the bouquet on the counter. She had no idea why Charlie might be there.

"I'm on my way back home to New Hampshire, but I was wondering if you might have a quick minute?"

Allie craned her neck to look at the clock behind the reception area.

"Sure, come with me." She brought Charlie to her office and offered her a seat.

"Thanks, but I don't want to keep you. You're a very good massage therapist, so I'm sure you're very busy. First, I want to apologize for all my yakking last night during my massage. I'm not sure where that all came from."

"No need to apologize." She wondered what Charlie wanted to talk to her about. She obviously liked the massage.

"I'm in Northland, and I was wondering if you could suggest a good massage therapist over in that area. If you know anyone. I asked the florist to leave my business card with the flowers, but I wasn't sure if they did." Charlie laughed. "Uh, I'm rambling again."

"I did see the business card, and I can't think of anyone off the top of my head in that area. But I'll ask around and email you." She thought Charlie looked uncomfortable. She was fidgety.

"I also left my card because…I don't even know if you're single, but if you are, I'd really like to have coffee or tea with you sometime. Northland's only forty-five minutes from here. I'm not usually this forward. I'm not usually this *anything* because it's been a long time since I've done this. But you already know that because I blathered on and on last night. I'm making a mess of this, aren't I. Sorry."

The whole thing with Geena and being catfished, then meeting the real person behind the photo, was exciting, but it was also confusing. Now right in front of her was an attractive woman who wanted to get to know her. Not jump into bed with her but get to know her.

"I'm very flattered, but—" She really was flattered, but she didn't go out with clients. Ever.

"I blew it, or you're married or in a relationship, or you're going to say if we met at a different time or different place…"

"No, I wasn't. And people only say those things in the movies and books. I don't think real people are that eloquent."

Charlie stood up. "I want to apologize. I had to take the chance. I haven't met anyone since I've been single again who sets off that spark of interest. And being my age, you don't waste chances. At least I try not to."

"I'm single." Allie stood up.

"Ouch."

"Oh no, I didn't mean it that way. I wanted to say I'm single, but because we saw each other as client and practitioner, even though it was one session, I wouldn't be able to date you for at least six months."

"Two people would know each other pretty well after six months, I think." Charlie smiled.

Allie returned the smile. Barb kept telling her she needed to start living. She felt like she was doing something behind

Geena's back, but that was ridiculous. They'd gone out once, and after the way Geena left, she knew she wouldn't ever get that call or text Geena promised.

She took a business card off her desk and handed it to Charlie. "Call me sometime. I'd like that."

CHAPTER NINE

Geena woke up to the sound of the kitchen bell and bright sunshine in her eyes. She hardly got any sleep last night—she'd replayed the day before and how it ended over and over. She figured she'd slept about two hours. Melissa was already up and out of the cabin to start her day in the camp's kitchen. She got dressed in a hurry because she could hear her group of campers making their way closer to the cabin, chanting her name while banging on something, but she couldn't figure out what.

"Geena, Geena, Geena."

It was the campers' job to wake up any oversleeping counselors and workshop teachers who didn't report to the dining hall before them. It was camp tradition to go back to your teacher's cabin, and by any means necessary—without entering or harming the cabin in any way—wake your counselor or teacher.

She opened her door as they approached the cabin.

"Nice drum." She pointed to the five-gallon plastic bucket and piece of a pine branch.

"C'mon, Geena, we're going to miss breakfast." They took off down the path to the dining hall. "She's awake! Let's eat!"

Geena followed, but she was distracted this morning. She tried to refocus her attention on her kids.

One day with Allie, and she'd somehow messed with her head or her feelings—she couldn't tell which. All she knew was she was up all night thinking about Allie's *feelings*, and not about how to get in Allie's bed.

She stepped up into the dining hall and grabbed a tray. There was no line. Everyone was already eating. Her group of kids cheered and clapped. "She's here! Yay!"

Scrambled eggs were plopped onto her tray.

"Sounded like you had a rough night," Melissa said. "Potatoes?"

Geena voice was barely a whisper. "Let's talk later, okay?"

"Later." Melissa put two pieces of burned raisin toast on her tray.

"Thanks a lot."

"You sleep in, you get the dregs, my friend."

Geena sat with her group and tried to make a show of eating even though she wasn't hungry. Her kids were going to set design this morning, and she had to prepare for several acting classes she was leading this afternoon. She went back to her cabin by way of the bathrooms so she could check her phone.

She shut the stall door behind her. The bathroom wasn't the most pleasant place to check her phone, but it was private and had the best signal because this bathroom was near the office. She had a text from Allie. *Thanks for the trapeze adventure.* Nothing else. She scrolled through her emails. Nothing. What did she expect? She'd practically run from the car when Allie said that she wanted to get to know her.

Still, her life was all over the web. Allie must have had a pretty good idea of who she was before she agreed to go on the trapeze adventure. Serial dater was practically her brand. Okay, she was pissed that her plan to seduce a really nice woman didn't work out. She'd done everything right. Allie should have been begging her to take her to bed. But instead she backed off.

Maybe Geena should come up with a different plan. She had to admit, Allie was different than the usual women she had sex with. Maybe what worked with those women wouldn't work with Allie. That thought had never occurred to her. Most of the women she had sex with were fans or casual hookups she met at events. Allie didn't even know who she was until the whole catfishing thing.

She answered some work emails, then sent Allie a text. *I'm sorry about the way our adventure ended. Try again? Can I make it up to you?*

Instead of preparing for the acting workshop, she spent the next hour googling *Allison McDonald* and *massage* and *Vermont* and *roller derby* trying to find out as much as she could about her. It looked like her Facebook page hadn't been updated for a couple of years, and it was pretty locked down. Her massage practice had a page on the Harvest Hill Wellness Center's site, but the *About* paragraph didn't tell her anything new.

But when she searched Vermont roller derby and found the Green Mountain Mavens of Mayhem team page, she sat down hard on the toilet seat. "Are you kidding me? Ms. Allie, you are not what you seem." She zoomed in on Allie in a short black skirt, black tights, tight black and green team tank, roller skates, a black and green helmet, and protective pads everywhere—knees, elbows, wrists. Her hands were on her hips. She looked tough. She looked incredibly hot. This one photo turned on its head nearly every assumption she'd made about Allie. She thought she was timid, introverted, a soft touch. But these photos showed a warrior woman who was obviously wicked competitive and a strong athlete.

She checked to make sure her phone was still muted and clicked on the two-minute video of the team titled "Mavens of Mayhem practice drills." She looked for Allie and wished she had her earbuds. She wasn't sure what was happening, but it looked like four skaters on a circular track were trying to block Allie from getting by. Then they were doing football-player-like drills while hopping on the toe stops of their skates. It was wild. Allie looked powerful. All the players had these crazy names on their backs. She paused the video and tried to read Allie's name. Mashley Whiplash? Who was this woman?

She found the team calendar and saw they had a match in Western Massachusetts this Saturday afternoon. Allie hadn't said anything about having a match this weekend. But she hadn't given Allie very much time to talk about herself, had she? Her stupid plan was what mattered during their trapeze adventure—seeing if she could get Allie into bed. That's all that usually mattered, but now she wanted to know more about Allie. Questions flooded her mind.

"Geena, you in your office?"

"Hey, Matty, I'll be right with you." Her first summer in camp, Matty had stopped outside the large building next to the kitchen and dining hall, pointed, and jokingly said, *There's your office*. He'd explained that some of the adults did keep their phones and took care of business in the bathrooms there. But it wasn't risk-free. If you got caught, your phone was taken away in a very public ceremony during story ring at campfire. In three years, she hadn't been caught.

She put her phone away and wondered what kind of favors she might have to do to get this Saturday afternoon and evening off. She wanted to see Allie skate more than she'd wanted anything in a long time. That wanting was dangerous territory that she'd spent years steering away from. She needed to snap out of it. The heat and loneliness were messing with her head.

❖

Allie looked at her phone after her final client of the day left. She scrolled through the notifications on her home screen and stopped at Geena's. She wasn't sure what to do. She'd hoped Geena would text back, but never thought she would.

"Al, I'm closing everything up, are you all set?" Mariah's voice startled Allie.

She opened her door and poked her head out.

"I'm done for the day. I'll be heading out soon. You can shut everything down—I'm all set."

"Okay, want to go get a grinder from Phil's?"

"Sure, let me tell Barb I won't be home for dinner, and I'll meet you over there."

She called Barb, who was delighted to have Allie bring her home one of Phil's grinders. She wasn't totally sure if she wanted to go through with the summer fling thing. She decided to go to Phil's and think things over, and if she still wanted to text Geena after that, she would.

She followed Mariah out of the building and drove to Phil's. Her stomach growled in anticipation of the best pepper steak and cheese sub she had ever tasted. Allie pulled into the parking lot and couldn't figure out how Mariah was already parked, out of her car, and in the diner. She found her at the table right inside the door.

"I'm starving, so I ordered for you—pepper steak bomb, right? Here's a Sprite."

"Thanks, I'm starving too."

"While we wait, why don't you tell me how things are going, kiddo? You've seemed distracted today. Barb okay? She didn't have a setback, did she? The animals okay? What's up?"

Allie wondered if all acupuncturists were like Mariah. No small talk—she got right to the point. She pictured Mariah with an acupuncture needle, approaching her thoughts.

"Does it have to do with the flowers that were delivered this morning? I know they were for you. Somebody trying to make up with you?"

"That's a lot of questions for a hungry person." Allie turned and looked at the counter to see if their order was up. Sometimes they called you, but sometimes they didn't. Phil's was like that.

"You're pretty centered, so the world tilts a skosh when you're not. I know you want to talk about it, whatever it is, because you wouldn't have come out with me if you didn't."

"You're right." She did want to talk with someone other than Barb, and Mariah was the most grounded person she knew.

"Of course, I am. I'm older than you and I'm always right."

"Number twenty-three!"

"That's us—I'll grab 'em," Mariah said.

Allie unwrapped and bit into her sub. She groaned and sighed at the same time.

She finished her first three bites before she started talking. "I always forget how good these are. I know you and Conrad have been together awhile, but how was it before him, when you were dating? How did you meet people?"

"Did you meet someone?"

"Maybe. Yes. Sort of? I don't want to say too much about it. Then I met this other person, who seems nice."

"That doesn't sound like a problem to me. Two women vying for your affection. Dating is hell. Especially up here in the hinterlands. I usually met people at work or at a party. Don't date anyone you work with. I know everyone says that, but don't. It's not someone from work, is it? Tell me all about it—I need to eat." She bit into her grinder.

"No, not really. One of them booked a massage at the B and B last night."

Mariah lowered her voice. "You're not considering dating a client, are you?"

"Not really."

"What is this *not really* stuff?"

Allie pointed to her mouth which was chewing and made a wait-a-minute sign.

"The woman was visiting Vermont. The massage was her first and last with me, and she told me she wanted to get to know me better. I told her I can't date a client, but because she was only my client once and wouldn't ever be my client again, we could get to know each other as friends, and after six months we could date if we wanted to go that route."

"Very professional. And so romantic." Mariah wiped her mouth with a paper napkin.

"I know, but she seems nice. She's older and very attractive. I don't have many friends here. But you think what I did is professionally okay? I wanted to run that by you." It felt okay to Allie, but she didn't want to look like she was being secretive about it. That didn't feel okay.

"And the other woman?"

"It's someone I shouldn't be attracted to, but I am. Nothing unethical. It's someone who doesn't want any of the same things I do long-term, but I'm not looking for long-term right now. I know that probably doesn't make any sense. She's... well, she's...something." Allie swore her lips could still feel that last kiss she and Geena shared before she bolted from the car. She felt her cheeks grow warm. She wanted to see Geena again. Maybe everyone needed to do one thing that didn't go along with their life plan. The thrill of just thinking that caused her heart rate to pick up speed.

"By the look on your face, she must be something indeed. You look all aflutter. No wonder you seemed off-kilter to me. You are. This woman has knocked you off your steady row."

"I wasn't going to talk about her. I really wanted your opinion on Charlie, the sort-of client." She rolled her grinder wrap into a ball and downed what was left of her Sprite. "Thanks. That was so good."

"No problem. I hope things get clearer for you. All I know is, you know when the right person comes along. At least I did with Conrad. We met at a friend's party, and that was it. We couldn't stop talking. It was different. It was easy for a change." Mariah got up from the table and grabbed Allie's trash. "I'll take it. Don't forget to take Barb's grinder, or she'll be fit to be tied. See you tomorrow."

"I totally forgot. That wouldn't have been pretty. See you." Allie went to the counter and asked for Barb's grinder that they were keeping warm. She waved to Mariah as she passed her on her way to her car. She leaned against her car and texted Geena. *I can think of several ways you could make it up to me.*

Her hands trembled as she started her car. She'd never done anything like this before. She dated, and either it went forward, or it didn't. Her problem was she always wanted forward to end in forever, even when the other person didn't. But this was different. They both wanted the same thing. She was going into this with her eyes wide open.

Her what-the-heck attitude faded as she drove home to Barb's farm. What had she done? She tried to convince herself that it was cold feet. She wasn't used to asking for what she wanted. She let other people lead and tell her what they wanted. She was starting to figure out the difference between being a caregiver and being a doormat. Geena either would or wouldn't get back in touch with her to set something up. She knew Geena didn't want a relationship, and she didn't want a relationship either. But her body wanted Geena. Her body was letting her know what it wanted every time she thought about getting together with Geena again. Was she confusing Geena with catfishing woman? Maybe. Maybe not. Did it matter? That was the confusing part.

❖

Geena waited for Melissa to get back to the cabin after dinner duty. She wanted to make sure she could get time off before making plans with Allie.

"Do you know anyone who would want to trade days off with me? I'm going into town Saturday and Saturday night."

"Hey, you practically pounced on me," Melissa said. "Everything okay?"

"There's a roller derby match I want to go to."

"Roller derby. That's a new one. You think the women will be easier to pick up there than a bar?"

"That Vermont woman is on the team."

"Oh, now it all makes sense. The complicated one. And the chase is on, as usual," Melissa said with a smirk.

"Yup, as usual." Nothing about this felt usual. But she couldn't allow herself to even utter those words out loud.

"What changed from the other night? I can't switch with you, but I think Tiffany was looking for someone to switch nights with."

"Awesome. Thanks." She kept thinking about that video

of Allie skating. She'd be a powerhouse in bed. She'd go to the game and try to meet up with Allie afterward to show her she came to the game to make up for her rude behavior the other day.

"I'm sure you'll have fun. You always do. Going to fire ring?"

"I think I'll look around for Tiffany first."

She watched Melissa head down the path toward the campfire. The door of the cabin next to theirs was open, and she knocked on the door frame. Tiffany was sweeping out the cabin and was very happy to switch days with her. Geena thanked her, then grabbed her towel and fresh clothes and headed down to the showers.

Before she got in the shower, though, she checked her phone hoping Allie had written back or left a voice mail or *something*. She wasn't sure why it mattered so much that she knew Allie was okay, but she felt unsettled not knowing.

She read the text twice. *I can think of several ways you can make it up to me.* She double-checked that the text came from Allie. Now she was even more confused. Allie was the one who put the brakes on, who stopped her plan in its tracks. Allie said she wanted to get to know her better, didn't she? Now Geena wondered what caused the change of heart.

She wanted to show Allie that it was the person using her photo who was nasty, not her. In return, Allie would be so charmed that she'd fall into bed with her. She knew Allie had gotten all hot and bothered in the car. And if—when—they had great sex, Allie would have an awesome memory to replace the hurt that person who catfished her gave her. The challenge excited her.

She didn't know how to answer the text. She knew she wanted to see Allie again. She would never admit to anyone, but she wanted to get to know her too. Something about

Allie found a space to get through her well protected facade to touch her, to make her remember who she was before all the games and conquests. She didn't have much time, and she typed four or five different texts before she settled on *I hope you'll describe them to me soon and in great detail. Maybe this weekend?*

Geena arranged her things in the shower stall, got undressed, and washed her hair, then took her washcloth and lavender soap and soaped her body, letting the warm water rinse her off. She shut off the water and toweled off inside the shower stall. She did her nightly tick check, then got dressed for bed.

Becoming Geena had enabled her to leave Virginia Harris and her vulnerabilities behind and be the someone who was wanted. Women wanted her, women thought she was beautiful and sexy, and being wanted, being desired was all that mattered. Or all that used to. Maybe Allie could be different.

❖

Allie texted a reply the next day, that she'd be down in Massachusetts on Saturday and near the theater camp, and it was too bad that Geena didn't have Saturday off.

Geena grinned to herself as she texted, *I switched. I'm available on Saturday. I can't wait to hear your requests.* This flirty dance came easy to her, but it rang slightly insincere when she did it with Allie. The reply came back immediately. Allie must be in town working. She wondered what Allie's town was like. And her cousin's farm.

Tell me where and I'll bring my list.

7pm at Barclay's Burgers in Coleridge? She chose Barclay's as a backup. Just in case things didn't work out with Allie, maybe Marcy would be around, either at the restaurant or the local bar where they'd met before a few times last summer. If Marcy wasn't around, she was sure there would be someone else at the bar.

The burger place?

Anyplace is fine with me as long as I'm sitting across from you.

You are very sweet. See you then.

She wondered why Allie still hadn't said anything about her roller derby match. And she wondered why she wasn't happy that Allie seemed to be moving in the direction she'd originally planned—into a bed with her. She still wanted to sleep with Allie, but now she had all these questions. She wanted to know why roller derby? Why did she move to Vermont? It had been so many years since she had allowed herself anything but a quick one-night stand or nooner with a woman, and this felt both exciting and scary. But she was still the one in control. She could choose how this went down.

CHAPTER TEN

Allie drove down Interstate 91 with her mind switching between the game ahead of her to seeing Geena again. She thought it couldn't have worked out better—she'd be seeing Geena right after the game, and maybe some of Mashley Whiplash would be lingering to give her the right attitude. Mashley was the official derby name that she formally chose a few weeks ago when she made the Mavens of Mayhem exhibition team. Once she learned the term *whip* for a technique skaters used when they allowed the momentum of another player to propel themselves forward, she knew it needed to be part of her name. The coach had her training to play the jammer position, and jammers used the whip often to get ahead and score points.

One night she and Barb were talking after dinner, and Allie was trying to come up with a name. She knew she wanted the word "whip" in there. Barb said it reminded her of the old *Rocky and Bullwinkle* cartoon villain, Snidely Whiplash. It was perfect. Allie wanted to sound tough and threatening to the opposing team. And she wanted to sound fast.

The Mavens played other second tier teams in the area, which gave them experience. Next year she'd be ready to try out for the official team, the Barre Bombers.

Allie pulled into the parking lot of the Thompson arena, grabbed her phone, and put her keys in a pocket of her gear bag. She hoisted her bag onto her shoulder and made her way to meet up with her teammates. As she walked through the parking lot and geared up mentally for the match, she felt Allie the massage therapist fade into the background and her alter ego, Mashley Whiplash, take over. Barb had helped her sew her name on her team tank, along with her number 19. She was so happy she'd found the derby. She loved everything about it—practice, her teammates, and bashing into players.

"Hey, Mashley! How's your hip?" Candy skated over to Allie's bench in the locker room.

"Better. Not as purple." She hiked up her skirt and revealed a purple and greenish bruise that covered a large part of her hip area.

"You rocked that corner, though, before you got slammed. You're the best jammer we've had. See you out there. Venus, you coming with me?" Candy latched on to the crook of Venus's arm and skated out of the room.

Allie laced up her left skate. She loved skating here, where it was okay to be a physically strong woman and use her strength and skill to push opposing players out of the way, while making her nasty Mashley faces. Thoughts of Geena took a back seat as she skated out to join the rest of the Mavens.

Her team greeted her with fist bumps and hip bumps.

"Let's skate the track," one of her teammates said.

They all skated around the oval marked out on the floor of the gymnasium. They skated flat track derby, and teams used whatever venues were available in their area. Team officials marked out the track with tape on the floor and would periodically check the tape during breaks in the action to make sure it hadn't lifted up or curled.

"It's a fast floor," Allie said.

After a couple of turns around, the other team skated around too, and then an official gave them a sign to get off the track. The announcer was ready to start things. Most derby matches had an announcer who introduced the players, promoted team swag, and gave the crowd newbies instructions on how a match was played.

When Allie had started watching derby videos online, she'd thought the announcer would break her concentration if she was a skater. But when she skated, she didn't notice the announcer or anything except the game. She was the jammer. It was her job to skate past the other team's pack of four blockers, and then come around the track again to score a point for every opposing team member she skated past. Her team's job was to both block the other team's jammer and help make a path for her to get through.

She scanned the crowd and saw a few familiar faces from Vermont before her name was called.

"Number nineteen, Mashley Whiplash!"

She put her mouth guard in and skated onto the track in full Mashley mode, fists raised, head nodding, and what she hoped was a sour, mean look on her face. She joined her teammates on the track for the short demo they gave before each match. Both teams skated around the track once, then lined up in formation like they would at the start of each jam. Mashley and the other team's jammer stood side by side a few feet behind the pack.

"See the two skaters standing back from the rest?" the announcer directed. "Those are your jammers—keep your eye on them during the jam. How do you tell them apart from the other skaters? They have a star on their helmet." The short, ponytailed, rumpled announcer had a wireless microphone and walked around near the head of the track as he spoke.

Allie and the other jammer pointed to the star on their helmets.

"Their job is to try to get through the pack."

Allie and the other jammer skated up to the pack and moved in slow motion, as the blockers from each team tried to block the opposing jammer and let their own jammer through.

"The first jammer to break through the pack is called the lead jammer. She can call off the jam at any point by tapping her hips with her hands." Allie's opponent skated through and demonstrated this for the spectators. "When the jammer comes around again and skates through the pack, that's when she'll score a point for each skater of the opposing team she passes. Got that, everyone? Keep your eye on the jammer. The ref in the center of the track will help you. He'll be pointing at the lead jammer as she skates. Are we ready?"

The crowd roared.

❖

Geena got to the arena a few minutes later than she wanted, and she tried to listen to the announcer as she made her way to an open spot on the bleachers. She wanted to have a good view of Allie or, rather, Mashley Whiplash. It looked like Allie was lining up with another woman behind the group of skaters. Then they started skating, and she had no idea what was happening or how they were scoring points. But she didn't care. She couldn't take her eyes off Allie. She bobbed and wove around other skaters, then broke free and bent low and skated really fast around the track to do it again. Then she would tap her hands on her hips and all the action stopped. The announcer brought the latecomers up to speed as the teams lined up again and changed out a couple of skaters.

Geena watched each jam leaning forward, her eyes

following Allie's every move. She felt her heart beat faster each time Allie broke free from the group of skaters, and she held her breath when opponents blocked her. Every turn around the track drew a circle around her heart, marking it taken.

After the end of the match the players stayed on the track and signed team swag and shook hands with people. Geena debated whether to go down or not and decided not to. She made her way out of the building and was stopped outside the doors by a tall woman in a torn Grateful Dead tank top, short shorts, and very large, unlaced Doc Martens, smoking a cigarette.

"Hey, are you Geena?"

"Yes, yes, I am." Geena didn't want to draw attention to herself today, so she'd worn an old pair of jeans and a plain blue T-shirt, put her hair in a ponytail, and wore very little makeup. She'd almost gotten away with it.

"Which team?" The skinny woman took a long drag off the cigarette and blew it out quickly.

"Excuse me?"

"Which team were you here for?" She took one more drag, then tossed the butt into the receptacle outside the doors.

"The Mavens of Mayhem?" Geena wasn't sure why the woman was asking or what the right answer might be.

"Me too. Great match, huh? It rocks my world when my team wins. Have you met them before? I know a few of the gals—let me bring you backstage." The skinny woman laughed a throaty laugh, then coughed.

"No, that's all right, I should get going." The plan was to meet Allie at the burger place. Allie didn't know she was at the game.

"You don't want to meet them? What's wrong with you?" The woman took a step toward her.

"Oh no, I'd love to meet them. Sure. Let's go." Change

of plans. She didn't want to piss off a fan and draw unwanted attention that way. She followed her back inside the building and through a door off the lobby.

"Not many people know how to get back here. I've got connections."

"Hey, thanks," Geena said, pretending to be impressed.

"No problem. Venus and Candy are gonna freak, man."

They walked down a hallway that felt damp and smelled like disinfectant and turned right into a large locker room with skaters talking and laughing.

"Everybody decent? It's Malorie, and I've got a surprise for Candy and Venus. Where are you?"

Geena continued to follow the woman—Malorie—around a row of lockers, as two players rushed toward them on skates, followed by a few more skaters...and Allie.

"Guess who this is?" Malorie exclaimed proudly.

Geena looked straight at Allie, whose lips were a thin line. She continued to look at Allie as she spoke. "My apologies, ladies. Malorie insisted I come back here with her to meet you. Your game was awesome. You were incredible." She didn't take her eyes off Allie. "This was my first roller derby game."

"We got ourselves a virgin, ladies." Someone behind Geena spoke.

Two women approached her.

"Oh my God—it's you, isn't it?" the first said.

"From online. That show," the second gushed. "Oh, I'm all nervous now. Venus, say something. It's Geena." She tried to hide behind Venus.

Geena saw Allie crack a smile and felt her shoulders relax. She didn't realize they'd been up by her ears.

"I'm Geena." She extended her hand to Venus.

"I'm Venus." She pointed over her shoulder. "And that's

Candy. She's, like, your biggest fan. We love your show. Thanks for coming to the match. Can I have you autograph something for Candy and me?"

"Sure thing. I don't think I have a pen, though. The match was great. You all look so fierce out there. I didn't realize how physical roller derby is. I'm a new fan, and I could watch your team all day—you have some amazing players. Do you call them players?"

Allie stepped next to Geena.

"Skaters. We're skaters. Nice to see you again, Geena."

Candy stepped out from behind Venus. "You know her? How come you never told me?"

Allie shrugged. "We just met a couple of weeks ago, and I didn't know you were a fan."

Geena added, "We're meeting up later for dinner, but I thought I'd surprise Allie."

"You did," Allie said.

Geena couldn't read what Allie's face was saying. She couldn't figure out why she couldn't wait to see a woman who made her feel all jumpy like this. Someone passed her a marker and a flyer from the match.

"To Venus and Candy?"

"Yes, thanks. Mashley, are you kidding me? You met Geena, and you didn't tell me?" Candy put her hands on her hips and pouted at Allie.

Geena wrote something on the back of the flyer and handed it to Candy, who read it out loud.

"*To Venus and Candy, the perfect duo of heavenly sweetness on wheels. Geena.* Thank you so much. I can't believe you're really here. Can you tell us, are you going to get together with Kimberly on the show? Will you come to more matches? We only have two left this summer."

Geena decided to do a Geena-like move for the women. She took off her cap and let her hair loose from her ponytail. Then she ran her fingers through her hair and shook her head so her long brown hair spread over her shoulders. She knew this was a good look for her, with or without makeup. She put her finger to her lips and leaned in toward Candy and Venus.

"I can't give away the secret."

She watched the skaters watching her. She knew they didn't know her at all. Like everyone else, they thought they knew Geena because they watched her show and read about her online, but they didn't know the real her, Virginia Harris.

Sometimes she didn't know how well she knew her anymore either.

Whenever she felt her confidence level drop or she felt uneasy about a situation, she knew she could be Geena, and her fans would prop her back up on the pedestal they put her on. The attention from Candy and Venus helped banish her wariness at not knowing what was going to happen tonight. She flashed another Geena smile at the two women.

"I'd love to watch you skate again. I hope it's sometime soon."

❖

When Allie first saw Geena behind Malorie—everyone on the team knew Malorie—she didn't know if she was glad to see her or not. It took her a minute to figure out that she had been there for the whole match. Then she thought, *What would the new Allie do?* She wouldn't act all put out. She'd be proud of herself for the way she skated, and she wouldn't act like Geena did her a big favor by coming to her match. No, Geena was the one who'd had the opportunity to watch her play and see what a badass she was. The new Allie would be okay with a one-nighter—in fact, she'd probably prefer a one-nighter. She flashed a smile at Geena.

"Got to grab my gear bag, and I'm all set."

Geena followed her to a bench at the other end of the room. Allie picked up her bag, turned around, and looked over Geena's shoulder to let her know she had two shadows with the names Candy and Venus. Geena turned to face them.

"Nice to meet you ladies. Hope to see you again. Thanks so much for watching the show."

"All set?" Allie wanted to take Geena's hand, but Candy had her phone out and was asking to take a selfie with Geena. Allie stepped away. She'd seen all the photos of Geena with this woman and that woman on her arm. There was a different woman in almost every photo. She didn't want to be one of them.

"Do you mind?" Geena asked her.

"No, go ahead."

Venus and Candy got their photos, and Geena followed Allie out of the building.

"Where are you parked?" Geena asked. "Do you want to follow me to Barclay's? It's right down the street."

"Is that why you chose Barclay's? Did you know I had a match today?" Allie stopped and looked at Geena.

"I did, but then I wondered why you didn't tell me. You look amazing."

The intensity of Geena's gaze caught her off guard. She started walking to her car again.

"Thanks. Let's not talk in the parking lot. The rest of my team are going to be coming out any second. I passed Barclay's on the way in. I'll meet you there. That's my car in the next row." Allie waved her hand at the cars in the lot.

"Hey, I'm parked in the same row."

She turned her head and looked at Geena. "You look pretty

great too." A picture of what they were probably going to be doing later flashed in her mind. She looked away. "There's my car."

"No way, I'm parked right next to you."

"Why would you park way back here? This is where the teams and officials and everyone connected to the match parks, so we won't take spaces from the paying customers. The hinterlands."

"I was a little late, and I pulled into the first space I saw. I didn't want to waste time looking for a space, but I didn't miss anything. You were doing that practice thing before the game."

"Match, and thanks for coming." She stopped next to her car.

"Right. Match."

Allie put her bag in the back seat. She closed the door, and when she turned around, Geena was only a few inches away.

Geena said, "I've been thinking about you. A lot. And all the ways I can make up for my bad behavior last time."

Geena's lips were inches from hers. She had been thinking about their kisses for a full week, and every cell in her body was screaming at her to kiss Geena. But not in the open parking lot where her teammates might see them, and worse, take pictures. She could feel her heartbeat. When she spoke, her words were almost a whisper. She tried to sound like she flirted like this all the time.

"That's all I've been thinking about." She touched her fingertip to Geena's lips, then moved away quickly. "I'll tell you all about it over dinner."

"I want details."

"Oh, you'll get details." She made an attempt at what she thought would be a badass move to get into her car. But her shorts caught on something, and she had to wrestle with the door and her shorts pocket for a second. Not sexy. She finally got into the car and shut the door. Her hands were shaking. "Be a grown-up, Allie, for crying out loud," she said under her breath. She watched Geena get into her car, started her own car, and followed.

CHAPTER ELEVEN

Geena thought she caught a glimpse of Marcy in the kitchen when they placed their orders at the counter. If it was Marcy and things didn't go the way she hoped they'd go, at least she knew she had a backup plan. It seemed like a solid plan, and she wouldn't be left on her own if Allie turned her down again. She pictured Allie skating around the track, her knees bent, grabbing on to the shirt of a teammate in front of her and using it to propel her forward. She pointed to a booth and they sat down.

"We're number forty-seven." She showed the paper ticket to Allie.

"Great. I'm always starving after a match." Allie patted her stomach.

"You look like you burn a lot of calories. Aren't you sore after? You skate with your knees bent. Ouch, my thighs."

"The first few weeks of practice when I started, I almost quit a couple of times because it was hard, and I was wicked sore. But the team is really great. We encourage each other and we especially encourage new players. I love it. I love them. But I don't want to talk about skating."

"What do you want to talk about, Allie?" Geena leaned forward.

Allie looked out the window for a second before she

spoke. She leaned forward as well and touched her fingertips to Geena's forearm.

"I want to talk about all the ways you're going to make up for last time. What I want you to do tonight."

She smiled at Allie, but it wasn't the same flashy smile she'd used on Candy and Venus. This was more than she expected. Allie had been thinking about her. More specifically, Allie had been thinking about having sex with her. She loved that.

"Can you tell me one way?" Geena touched the back of Allie's hand and traced a small line up and down.

"I want you to undress me."

"You do?" She definitely wanted to take Allie's clothes off.

"Yes."

"Slowly?" She pictured herself hooking her thumbs in the waistband of Allie's shorts and hiking them down over her hips. She didn't usually get so worked up before sex.

"No."

She decided to go for it. "I'd like to do that right here, right now."

"Number forty-seven!" Both women jumped, then laughed.

"Sorry," Allie said.

Was Allie blushing? Geena said, "Nothing to be sorry about."

"We were in another world for a minute, or something."

"Or something. I'll get the food." Between thinking about Allie all week, seeing her at the derby, and now sitting across from her, Geena couldn't remember the last time she was this aroused with her clothes on.

❖

Allie watched Geena walk to the counter, grab a tray of food, and walk back. She didn't feel like eating a burger right now. She wanted Geena, but how would she feel tomorrow or the next day when there was no Geena? They could have the rest of the summer. She wanted to let go and enjoy it. Her body certainly felt ready to do that. Her mind was almost there.

"Here you go—a bacon cheeseburger and fries for you, and the double Barclay burger for me." Geena laid out the food in front of them and brought the tray back to the counter.

She found it difficult to look anywhere but at Geena, and whenever she looked, Geena was looking right back at her.

"Congratulations on a great win." Geena lifted her burger in toast fashion and touched it to Allie's burger. "Should we continue our conversation about your clothes and how you want me to remove them?"

She tried to focus on chewing her bite of burger and washed it down with her ginger ale. They didn't really know each other at all. They'd had a couple of conversations, exchanged a few texts, that's all. But Geena's message had been loud and clear when she all but ran from the car the last time they were together. She was very clear that she didn't want to get to know Allie. She only wanted some fun while she was here for the summer.

"You almost made me choke on my burger."

"Sorry. I'll concentrate on finishing mine so we can get out of here."

"I'm not as starving as I thought I was."

"Oh, I think you're pretty hungry from what I remember from our last time together. That's all I've been thinking about." Geena put down the rest of her burger.

Allie was aware of every breath she took and tried to slow

her breathing. The thought of Geena at camp, thinking of how they kissed and wanting her, made her forget any questions she had about how well they knew each other or what their plan might be after tonight. She wanted Geena. She pretended again to be someone who did this all the time.

"Do you have somewhere in mind? You seem to know the area pretty well."

"If you don't mind," Geena pulled out her phone, "I want to check on a place."

Allie ate some fries while she waited for Geena to finish. She was glad that Geena surprised her at the match. It caught her off guard, and she didn't have time to get anxious about tonight. She figured Geena knew the area so well because she probably did this with lots of other women. But she didn't care about that right now.

"We're all set. You can leave your car here if you want, and we can drive over together."

"Where are we going?"

"There's a cute place on a lake that has these little cottages. I booked one for tonight. But before we go…" Geena put her phone back in her pocket and reached for one of Allie's hands. "Tell me one more way I can make things up to you."

"Really?" Allie glanced around at the now full restaurant. She was relieved that no one here seemed to know Geena.

"Yes. No one can hear us."

"I want you to kiss me." She could almost feel Geena's lips on hers again.

"Before or after I take your clothes off?"

"Both."

"All of a sudden I'm hungry again, but not for food."

She loved the way Geena was looking at her. It emboldened her. "Thanks for coming to my match." She reached across the table and took Geena's hand.

"You have such beautiful eyes. You really look at me," Geena said.

Geena reached over and touched her cheek with a tip of a finger. The expression on Geena's face changed from playful to something else. Softer. Then it changed right back to playful. Well, okay. She could be playful too.

"Can we go to that cabin now?" Allie took her keys and got out of the booth. "I'll follow you."

"Ride with me. It's only about fifteen minutes from here."

"This parking lot looks a little sketchy. I don't want to leave my car here."

Geena smiled. "Okay, keep an eye on my rear."

"My pleasure."

❖

Geena went into the building marked *Office* and checked them in, then motioned to Allie to follow her car. They pulled in front of a tiny white cottage with dark green trim and parked. She'd been here before with a few women when she was at camp. She had a plan for tonight like she did for every time she went out with a woman. Most women were ready to do anything she asked right from the start, so she always tried to surprise them in some way, make things more interesting for herself. Things with Allie were going better than expected. Better than she hoped, actually. Allie seemed to have changed her mind about having fun with her this summer. The funny thing was that all through dinner, more and more questions about Allie kept popping into her head. How long had she lived at her cousin's farm? Where was she from? How long had she been a massage therapist? That wasn't in the plan. The sound of Allie's car door brought her out of that.

She got out of her car and opened the door to the cottage. It smelled a little piney and woodsy, and a bit like cinnamon. She flipped the light switch, and two small ceramic beer steins that someone had converted into bedside lamps glowed on either side of the bed.

"This is very cute," Allie said.

"You're very cute." Geena put her hands on Allie's hips. "I think I remember someone saying something about wanting me to kiss her?" She stepped closer to Allie. Those eyes. They made all her usual lines get all mixed up in her head.

"That was me," Allie said softly.

"So it was." She kissed her, moved her hands to the small of Allie's back, and drew her closer.

Allie's kiss met hers and woke a part of her that she had put in hibernation long ago. A small burst of panic made her hesitate for a second, but everything about this felt so right and so good. She didn't want to stop. Allie's hands ran up her back and pulled her even closer. She felt herself following Allie's lead. None of her weeklong mental preparation for this night had gotten her ready for this.

She was used to being the one who led the way. The women she was with usually had made up a fantasy about what Geena would do to them, and she was happy to make those fantasies come true. She didn't know what to do with this. Her heart pounded and her knees were threatening to give out. She'd read about people being kissed like this but didn't think it was for real. What was happening to her body right now was very real. And she was having trouble remembering her next line.

❖

Every place Geena touched her came alive with desire and made her want more. Allie usually tried to anticipate what a partner wanted and gave her that and followed along. She thought if she did that, the woman would want her more and love her more. It wasn't that she was ignoring cues from Geena, but this encounter was like some wild dance that they both already knew the steps to. She was definitely leading more often than not, and Geena's responses fueled her longing.

She whispered in Geena's ear, "I need to get these clothes off. Now." She started to pull off her tank top. She liked following her own desires.

Geena pulled back and looked at her with hungry eyes. "I think that's my job tonight."

"I want you." All she could think about was making love with Geena. "Well, then do it. Take them off."

Allie lifted her arms up and Geena took off her tank top, then her bra, then quickly moved to unbutton her shorts. She helped Geena slide them down, then pulled off her shorts and underwear. On her way back up, Geena ran her hands up the outside of her legs and stopped at her hip.

"That's some bruise." Geena's fingertips grazed her skin.

"Hazard of skating. Ignore it. Hardly hurts at all anymore." Nothing hurt right now.

Geena took both her hands, led her to the bed, and kissed her.

She tried to get them both onto the bed gracefully, all the time kissing without stopping, but they ended up tumbling onto the bed laughing.

"You have the best laugh," Allie said.

"You look incredible."

"Do you like this outfit?" She liked having fun with Geena.

"I really like this outfit." Geena climbed onto the bed and ran a finger down Allie's arm, hip, and thigh.

"I think you might have one that's something like mine." She reached for Geena's T-shirt, but she gently pushed her hand away.

"I'm supposed to be making up for my behavior, and I want all the focus on you, beautiful Allie."

"So I'm going to lie here all naked and everything and you're—"

"I'm going to kiss you." Geena bent her head down. "Here. And here. And over here." Her lips lingered on Allie's skin, and then they followed her fingertips up to Allie's mouth.

Allie kissed her and stroked her face.

Geena's hand moved down her back and around her hip, and tried to move between her thighs. Allie's breath caught, and she opened her legs. She reached for Geena, grabbed her shirt, and twisted it in her hand.

Geena pulled away. "Whoa, hang on there."

"Sorry." Allie sat up and pulled the cotton spread around her. Geena was clearly irritated with her. Was this how Geena was in bed with women, fully clothed, but never fully involved? She knew Geena kept people at a distance—she'd seen how Geena was with her fans. Maybe that was how she was with everyone all the time.

❖

Geena sat up in bed next to Allie. She couldn't believe what a mess she'd made of tonight. She'd felt off after that burger, but didn't want to disappoint Allie. She wasn't feeling any better—if anything, the grumbling in her stomach was now lower. She kept trying to ignore it. The whole night was planned in her head, beginning to end like usual, but that burger, then that incredible kiss, knocked everything out of balance. That's how she felt. Way out of balance.

The feelings that came up when they kissed and touched were so foreign to her but felt so right. Everything about Allie felt so right. And now she'd totally screwed everything up. What was she supposed to say now?

"Ugh. I don't feel well. It started a little while ago—must have been my burger. But I still wanted you to have a good time. I never want to let a woman down in that department, and I definitely didn't want to let you down. Plus, I didn't want to miss out on my chance to kiss you everywhere. And I mean *everywhere*." She looked Allie up and down. "Have I told you I love kissing a woman's *everywhere*?" She smiled her best Geena smile at Allie. "I wanted you to have a good time."

"I'm sorry you're not feeling okay, but you should have said something. It's okay. We could have just hung out or something."

No matter what the words were, Allie looked disappointed and kind of sad. It bothered her to see Allie like that. But the thought that skipping sex, just hanging out, would have been fine with Allie bothered her even more. She watched Allie get up from bed and put her clothes on.

"Hey, come back here."

"Don't worry. Your record is still clean. You didn't let me down at all."

"Allie, I'm sorry. I think what I said came out the wrong way." She didn't like the way things were headed. This wasn't part of the script. She could always charm her way out of almost anything with women. But she always chose women she knew she could charm easily. Allie was different. As she thought those words, the panic that had been hovering in the background all night moved front and center. Her stomach was more settled now, but she was still not feeling great. She tried to get back on script.

"Don't sit in the chair. Come back to bed with me. Let's

turn out the lights and get cozy." She got up from the bed and went to Allie's side. "Let me get you under the covers. We can make out a little. Kiss a little. I thought about your lips all week, and when you kissed me tonight, it was more than wonderful. Let's kiss some more."

"But you don't feel well. That doesn't feel right. Can I get you something? They must have a soda machine here somewhere. Can I get you a Coke or a ginger ale for your stomach?"

"Sure. A Coke would be great. I think right outside the office is a machine." So now Allie was in the lead again. Nothing was going like she'd planned. And no matter what Allie said, she knew she was disappointed.

Allie checked her wallet. "I'll be right back."

CHAPTER TWELVE

She found the Coke machine and fought back tears that brimmed in her eyes. The one time in her life that she'd said to hell with it and decided to have fun, and the night went all to hell. This time it wasn't because she was moving too fast in a relationship—there was no relationship. She wanted to believe that it was only Geena's stomach that was bothering her, but her intuition told her that something else was going on.

She made her way back to the cottage and gave Geena the can of Coke.

"Thanks so much. Can we talk for a minute?"

"Sure. I know we really don't know each other very well. I know that's all part of this—we're a summer sex adventure. But before we talk, can I ask you something, and will you tell me the truth? We aren't in a relationship, so there's nothing to lose by telling me the truth, right?" She brought a chair next to Geena's and sat down.

"Right, I guess. Go ahead."

"Is your stomach really bothering you, or did I do something that made you decide not to have sex with me?" She hoped Geena would tell her the truth.

Geena looked around the room and let out a deep sigh before she spoke. She looked directly at Allie. "I was telling you the truth before when I said my stomach was upset. The Coke is helping. Really, Allie. You're perfect." Geena leaned forward and took her hand. "Incredible, sexy, funny, and fierce."

She watched Geena look away from her and felt her hold her hand a little tighter.

Geena continued, "I've never met anyone like you. I googled you, for crying out loud. I don't google women. I thought about tonight all week, and I kept telling myself that you sounded like you were all in for a fun night of sex, I would be making up for my behavior last time, and maybe if I was lucky you'd want to have sex with me a couple more times before the summer was over." Geena shifted in her chair so her legs hung over the arm. "When we were eating dinner, I kept wanting to ask you questions like we were on a date, like a real date. But I don't do that. So I want to make sure you know that tonight is all on me. My head wasn't in the right place, and I don't feel okay, and I messed things up. Oh, and I'm also not used to talking with women like this."

As Geena talked, Allie thought she saw the flashy, always on web star retreat to the background and a softer, more real version of Geena sat across from her, picking at a loose thread on the chair as she spoke. She saw flashes of this more vulnerable side beneath the flirty, confident, sexy actress. It reminded her of herself when she skated. For whatever reason, it was so much easier to access the fierce, competitive side of herself when she had her uniform with her derby name, Mashley Whiplash, across her back. As she listened to Geena, part of her knew she could never just have sex with this woman. She tried to banish that thought from her mind. Because she could certainly *try* to just have sex.

"You're doing fine." She continued to hold Geena's hand. "I believe you."

"You do? Really?"

"Shouldn't I?"

"Well, yes, I'm telling you the truth, but you don't act like a lot of the women I've been with. You're so nice all the time. In a genuine way."

"Not all the time, once you get to know me."

"I think I'd like to do that."

"Do what?"

"Get to know you better."

The words made her heart beat faster. That was what she wanted too. Allie looked hard at Geena's face. She wasn't joking around. She was serious.

"What does that mean to you?" She wasn't going to be the one to define this. She always did that for women she dated and said what she thought they wanted to hear.

"I don't know," Geena admitted. "I haven't had much practice at it. I'm not going to say I want to be friends with you, because I don't think I could ever only be friends with you. When we kiss, I don't know how to explain it, but it's like we know each other. Does that sound crazy? Is it just me?"

She was so glad Geena said that first. So often her feelings were not in line with what the other person was feeling. She often convinced herself that a relationship was more than it truly was, because she wanted a long-term relationship.

"It's not just you. I felt it too." But the fact that both Geena and Lauren—who looked exactly like Geena in her head— were excellent at flirting didn't help her sort things out either.

"Should I ask you out on a date?" Geena let go of Allie's hand, flipped her legs off the arm of the chair, and moved to the edge of her seat.

"I'd like that. I think you should."

Geena stood and took Allie's hand again. "Allison, would you like to go out with me on a date?"

Allie stood up too. "Yes, I would, Geena." She tried to sound formal but couldn't keep from smiling. Geena was beaming a smile right back at her.

"It would have to be next Sunday, on my night off. Would you want to meet up in Brattleboro again?"

"Do you mind driving a bit farther? There's a great barbecue place a little north of Brattleboro. Do you like barbecue?"

"Love it. Sounds great. But we have to figure out a better way to communicate. I can't always check my phone, and you don't have service most of the time. I'm usually free for a while right after dinner at camp, unless there's an emergency or we're having a show."

"And I'm usually still in town most nights, because I have some clients at night. How about six?"

"That's too early for me. Can you do later?"

"I'm always done by eight."

"I can do eight most nights. But if you don't hear from me, it's because I'm doing camp type things."

"And if you don't hear from me, I either didn't have clients or my cousin needed me at home."

Allie gave Geena directions, and they confirmed a time for the following Sunday. She felt Geena's arms around her. That conversation didn't go at all how she expected. Nothing about Geena was what she expected.

❖

"It's probably too late for you to drive all the way home." Geena ran a line of light kisses up Allie's neck. She needed to do something to take her mind off what she'd done. She'd made a real date with a woman she liked. She was excited and more than a little panicky. She couldn't get over the fact that

Allie didn't have the expectations that other women did when they were with her. It made her irresistible. She didn't want Allie to drive home. She wanted to spend the night with her. She felt Allie respond to her kisses.

"I'm glad you're feeling better, but I think I'll get going soon," Allie said. "Part of me wants to stay, and part of me thinks that if we have sex tonight, I might never see you again."

That hit too close to home. How could Allie not know her, but know her so well? If she was honest, she'd have to admit that there was a good chance that's exactly what would happen. The sex would be great, and then she'd go back to camp and probably be in a total panic and cancel the date.

"I'll share the rest of your Coke with you before I leave, though." Allie ended the sentence with a kiss that made her toes curl and had her wanting to say yes to whatever Allie asked of her.

"I'd be happy to share my Coke with you."

She passed the can to Allie and sat back down in the chair. Allie turned her chair to face her. Geena thought she could look at her all night.

CHAPTER THIRTEEN

This wasn't how Allie thought tonight would go at all. She was listening to Geena tell her how she was hired to work on *Days and Nights*, but her body was still sending signals that it wasn't happy she wasn't spending the night with Geena. Okay, she had to admit she liked sitting across from her and sharing stuff about their lives. And she could tell by the color of Geena's face that she wasn't feeling terrific. As much as she wanted to take off her clothes again and jump Geena, having sex tonight now felt like a gamble she didn't want to take.

"Do you get to pick out the clothes you wear on the show?" She took a sip of Coke and passed the can to Geena.

"In a way, yes. Most of them come from my closet."

"They don't give you clothes? I thought there were wardrobe people."

"You've seen too many movies. It's a pretty skinny operation. That's why I do other things besides the show."

"What kind of things?"

Geena sat up and moved to the edge of her seat. "You'd be surprised." She laughed. "Don't look at me like that. I knit."

"You knit? Really?" She was having a hard time picturing Geena in a peaceful pose, knitting. She seemed too full of energy. "That's so interesting." She liked that a little color was back in her face. She looked like she was feeling better.

"I know, I know. It doesn't go with the image, does it? You must have seen photos of that online—I knit on set sometimes. But holding knitting needles isn't as exciting as holding another woman, so maybe those don't come up right away when people search. I knit hats, and mittens, and gloves, and some other stuff, and sell them in my sister's Etsy shop. And I do some public appearance stuff that I get paid for."

Allie thought about it. "You're right, it doesn't fit your image, but I'm glad you told me. I assumed you were living the life of the rich and famous. I didn't know."

"Unless you're in the business, most people don't know. I have an agent, and she tells me about gigs I might be interested in. Most of them don't happen. I've done a couple of small things in television, but that was before the Geena phenomenon."

"Have you always wanted to act?"

"Hey, I think it's my turn to ask questions now. Have you always wanted to be a massage therapist?"

That smile saved Geena again, Allie thought. But not before she saw Geena's expression shut down. She smiled back. Geena moved farther back into her chair, creating more physical distance between them.

Allie pretended not to notice the shift and decided it was her turn to open up. "I graduated with a business degree and had a series of okay office jobs. The money wasn't bad. This was while I was living in Massachusetts." She saw Geena's raised eyebrows. "That's where I'm from, where my parents lived. Anyhow, I was going through a rough time, very stressful, and on doctor's advice I visited a massage therapist. It was my first time, and on my drive back home all I could think of was that was what I wanted to do. I love it." She put her feet onto the chair and drew her knees up and hugged them. "I feel so lucky that I found the thing I was meant to do. Can I have another sip of Coke?"

"Sure." Geena passed her the can. "I'm from Massachusetts too. I mean, that's where the series is filmed, but it's also where I grew up. Over by the coast, about a half hour north of Boston. Where did you live?"

"All over Massachusetts. We didn't stay in one place very long. But I always loved going to Barb's farm for holidays and sometimes in the summer. Barb's parents, my aunt and uncle, left the farm to her after they passed away, and it always felt like home to me. After my parents died, I sold their house and came to Vermont, first to help Barb, then to open my business. It felt like coming home. It's a great life."

"I can tell from your face how much you love it—your eyes sparkle when you talk about your life there. Have I told you that you have the most stunning eyes I think I've ever seen?" Geena leaned forward again and removed the Coke can from Allie's hand.

She felt warmth rise in her face under Geena's intense gaze. "Yes, I think you might have."

When Allie talked about her life, Geena seemed to relax. She didn't think Geena was all that comfortable talking about herself and her acting. Her answers sounded like she was being interviewed by some blogger. But she seemed very comfortable throwing her a line and watching her reaction.

Her breath caught as Geena reached toward her face and traced a line along her hairline, behind her ear, and down her neck to her collarbone. She took Geena's hand and gave it a quick kiss.

"That's my cue to get on the road, I think." She tried to get up from the chair, but Geena's knees were in her way.

"You think? Are you sure?" Geena got up and moved so

Allie could get up. They'd pushed their chairs so close together the cushions almost touched.

She took her keys from the small table by the door of the little cottage. "I'm sure. Tonight's been great." She wanted to go on that date with Geena, even if it was the only one.

"Not all of it. I could make it better. I think we both know that. Do you want to sleep over? We could turn out the lights and snuggle." Geena took her hands in hers.

"We simply had a few little bumps. That's nothing. And do you really think I believe we would only snuggle? What are we, old married people?" The minute that sentence left her mouth she regretted it.

"You're right. We'll text. And I'll see you next weekend for barbecue. It'll be fun." Geena touched Allie's arm and opened the door.

There had been a 360-degree change in the weather in that room, Allie thought as she walked to the door. She wasn't going to let the night end that way. Geena had gone from flirting with her again to retreating again. What would the new Allie do? She'd give Geena something to think about all week long—that's what she'd do. She put one arm around Geena's waist and pulled her close and kissed her. And kissed her again. The desire she'd kept at bay during their conversation sprang to life again, and she didn't hold any of it back when she kissed Geena a third time. Then she gave her a quick hug.

"I *can* be lots of fun. See you next weekend. I can't wait. Thanks for tonight. It really was wonderful." She had to talk in short sentences because she was breathless from kissing her.

Geena didn't say anything for a few seconds. Allie thought she looked a bit gobsmacked. She liked that she could have the effect on her. She liked it a lot.

"Um…yeah." Geena nodded her head. "Was wonderful. See you, Allie."

❖

Geena watched Allie's car leave the parking area and kept watching her taillights for as long as she could see them through the trees. She tried to sort out how she was feeling but couldn't latch on to a thought long enough to actually think about it. Allie was in her head. Allie was in the cottage. In the chair where she sat, over on the bed, inside that can of Coke. She was everywhere. She lay on the bed and put her head on Allie's pillow. It still smelled like her. Things hadn't turned out quite like she thought they would for a second time. She turned onto her back and looked at the acoustic tile ceiling and remembered when she was in school, how she would count the dots on one tile, over and over again, so she wouldn't cry when her parents didn't show up for one of her school plays. She felt a little like crying now, but this was so different.

She wanted to sort out what was going on with Allie. When they were together, every plan she made to seduce Allie got turned around and upside down. She had waited all week to see her, and the time had gone by too fast. And now she'd have to wait another whole week to see her.

This was new. She usually couldn't wait to get rid of a woman once they'd had sex. But she and Allie hadn't had sex—maybe that's what had her all messed up. Getting rid of Allie never came into her mind. She fiddled with the bedspread and turned her face to the side to breath in Allie's scent again.

She loved talking with Allie. True, Allie got a little too close with her questions, but she loved hearing about Allie's life and what she liked and how much she loved her life in Vermont. She couldn't remember when she'd stopped thinking of a future that included a woman. One woman. Sometime after her two years of college, when the local modeling jobs she got into morphed into community theater and paid gigs, and women started fangirling around her. After a photographer started calling her *Geena* instead of *Ginnie* and her agent found out about it and said, *It goes with your Italian heritage, your mother's Italian, right? What's not to like. It's a great name. People will love it.* Her agent was right. She got more job offers after she changed her name. Then she became Geena and left Virginia at her parents' house.

She couldn't keep up her Geena persona more than a handful of times with any one woman, and she was afraid to let anyone see who she really was, inside or outside. Allie didn't seem to care about her fandom, even after she found out who she was. Allie had contacted her because she was a nice person and wanted to make sure she knew someone was out there using her photo to catfish women.

From what Allie told her, she'd been pretty hung up on that online imposter and the photo she'd used. Maybe Allie wasn't like the fans who wanted to have some fantasy come true, but maybe she was still confusing that online relationship and the image of Geena with Geena herself. She'd have to be careful. Maybe Allie was more like the fangirls after all.

CHAPTER FOURTEEN

The week went by faster than Allie thought it would, fueled by several visits to a nearby mountain retreat center after two of their massage therapists quit. She knew why after only two visits and refused to come back. They overbooked their spa services and it was like an assembly line. It made her appreciate the small, well-managed Wellness Center in Proctor's Falls.

Her eight o'clock phone calls with Geena were the perfect end to her day. They had talked three times during the week. She'd missed one night because she was at the retreat center, and Geena missed one. During each phone call, she tried to ask Geena questions that wouldn't make her pull back into herself. She always seemed a little guarded at the start of their conversations, but once they talked for a few minutes, she seemed more relaxed.

The phone calls were a good idea, she thought. It helped her see the difference between Geena and Lauren. They were nothing alike. She liked the flirty, sassy, overconfident Geena that she saw when she was around fans or trying to use a line on her. But she was more than captivated by the quiet, gentle, thoughtful woman she was getting to know over the phone.

"You're in dreamland again." Barb tapped the edge of her plate with her fork.

"I'm sorry, I was thinking about—"

"Geena the actress. You've been up on that nine cloud all week. You usually talk about the team when you come home from practice. You're not counting chickens, are you?" Barb took a long sip of her iced tea.

"No, she's not looking for a relationship—she told me that the first time we met. And I'm not going to pretend she'll change. I did that before, and I promised myself I would never do it again. What's that saying? Believe what people tell you when they tell you who they are, or something like that?"

"That's close. The very smart Maya Angelou said something along those lines. Oh, I forgot"—Barb snapped her fingers—"you got something in the mail today. I'm done. I'll get it for you." Barb took her plate to the sink.

"I'm done too. What is it?" She put her plate and utensils in the sink and started to put the leftovers in containers.

"A card, I think. I'll take care of the dishes if you finish with the food. Want to play some cards after out on the deck?"

"Sure, but I've got a phone call at eight. Didn't Connie want you to come into town and go to the movies this weekend?" She put the card on the kitchen table and finished with the leftovers. Sometimes she worried that Barb spent too much time by herself up here on the hill since her surgery.

"We're going tomorrow afternoon. I had a social life before you came up to live here, you know. I've lived here all my life. I go through spells of wanting to stay closer to home, and then I go through spells of needing to get into town or to go over to New Hampshire. Connie's not worried about me— don't you be either. Okay?"

"Okay." She picked up the card. "I wonder who this is from?"

"It's New Hampshire on the return address, but no name."

Allie opened the envelope and the card.

"Oh gosh. I'm taking this out on the deck."

"Everything okay?"

"Everything's fine." She picked up her iced tea and picked up a cribbage board and deck of cards from the shelf by the door on her way out. The card was from Charlie, the woman who'd brought flowers to the Center. There was a letter inside the card. It was a nice letter, about her life in New Hampshire, her job, things she liked to do. She asked some questions about Allie too. Charlie said she knew it was old-fashioned, to write a letter, but she thought it was less intrusive than a phone call or an email. She'd found Allie's address online.

Charlie was very up-front about what she wanted in the future. She wanted to share her life with someone again. Allie looked out toward the barn and brought up a picture of Charlie in her mind. She remembered short salt-and-pepper hair and kind brown eyes. She was quite a bit older than Allie. That was probably why she knew what she wanted and was so direct about it, she thought.

Allie didn't know if she wanted to write her back or not. She slid the card back into its envelope and put it aside. Then she put the pegs in the cribbage board and shuffled the deck while she waited for Barb.

❖

Geena finished her dinner and stopped by the arts and crafts building to check out the set design for the plays at the camp during the next few weeks. A few of the kids were moving pieces on and off the stage. There were campers from age eight to eighteen, and they performed three plays at the end of each summer, one on each weekend in August, and camp ended for each group after their play.

"Those look fantastic—you did such a great job! I can't believe you got them all done ahead of schedule."

Geena's group of campers were between thirteen and fifteen and were working on *Victoria Martin: Math Team Queen*.

"I'm so excited that we get to go first this year. Only one more week," said Madison.

"Eight days from today you'll be standing right here," Geena said. "Doing youth theater at home has really helped you grow as an actor."

"You think so?"

Madison, the lead, helped wheel a large chalkboard across the stage with Ethan, another actor. All the kids worked on every part of the production, and counselors facilitated in their areas of experience. She worked with all three groups of kids with rehearsals, stage direction, and voice projection.

Working at the camp let Geena combine two of her favorite things—helping to make a safe space for LGBTQ kids to be themselves, and being involved in theater. Drama club in high school had saved her life. It gave her the family she didn't have at home. She missed the camaraderie of the theater and the rehearsals. On her web show there were no rehearsals. She was expected to know her lines when she got to the set. She liked everyone on set, but it wasn't the same as the theater. Performing in front of a live audience fed her, like vitamins for her soul. But she couldn't pay her rent with theater work.

She hung out with the kids until it was a little before eight and time to call Allie, then walked down the path to the restroom. Her hands were a little clammy, and she rubbed them on her shorts. There was a little zing of racing butterflies in her stomach when she pulled out her phone. Each time she spoke with Allie this week made her want to talk to her more and spend more time with her. And the odd thing was, it didn't feel as scary as she thought it would.

Allie answered after the first ring. "Hi." She sounded breathless.

"Hi, yourself. You sound like you've been running up a hill. I've missed you," she whispered.

"I've been playing cribbage with Barb, and I forgot to take the phone out to the deck with me. I didn't want to miss your call."

"You didn't?" She loved teasing Allie a little bit. She loved hearing Allie tell her that she missed her and wanted to talk to her all night. It was so different from the women who loved her character on *Days and Nights*. They wanted to talk to her all night and be with her any way Geena wanted, and it did give her ego something to chew on, but the satisfaction was temporary.

"No, I didn't. I've waited all day to talk to you and hear about your day at camp. And to tell you I can't wait to see you Sunday. It's been a long week."

"It's been a very long week. Camp was good today. We had a good rehearsal this morning with the little kids, and two that were a little bumpy this afternoon, but we all had fun. There's a girl who's the lead in *Victoria* who reminds me of me at that age." As soon as that piece of information was out of her mouth, she wished she could take it a back. "I always want these few weeks during the summer to be a safe place for these kids. Where all the adults are caring and loving and accepting, and the rules for behavior are respected by everyone. I think it helps that they don't have their phones. Well, most of them don't. I think there's a few that do. How are the hills of Vermont today?" Well, that sounded like a line from a really bad play. *Well done Geena.*

"The hills are pretty green. You are so sweet."

"I don't know if anyone has ever told me I was sweet."

"Like candy I want to eat."

"Allie." It would be so easy to respond with more flirting and teasing, but she remembered what Allie had told her about phone calls and the catfishing woman. "We promised we weren't going to do that on the phone, and I think it was you who made us promise, because you said it would remind you of that online creep who was using my picture. Besides, I'm sitting on a toilet in a camp bathroom. You're all cozy up on the farm. It's probably a log cabin surrounded by pine trees."

"You're right, we promised. I'm usually not like that. I'm usually the practical one, but when I'm around you, I want to play. Okay"—the tone of Allie's voice changed—"I'm all business now. We don't live in a log cabin. It's an old farmhouse, with a barn out back, but there are very tall pine trees out back. They're the reason we don't have cell service. I saw a few of my regular clients today, picked up a couple of books at the library for Barb and me, had supper, and played a couple of games of cribbage with Barb. She won, the stinker."

"I'd like to see your farm someday." The words came out before she could stop them. They'd only seen each other three times. It seemed too early, but was it? This was all new territory for her.

"I've got an idea," Allie said. "But before I tell you, we can still stick to our original plan for tomorrow if this doesn't sound like it'll work. The farm is about another twenty-five minutes north of Curtis's Barbecue in Putney. You could drive straight up to the farm, and I could grill some burgers for us. If you play your cards right, I might even slap some barbecue sauce on them. It won't come close to Curtis's by a mile, but then you'd know where I live."

The toilet seat was suddenly even more uncomfortable.

She stood up in the stall and wanted to pace, but that wasn't happening. She sat down again and stood right back up, then turned around like she was looking for an escape hatch.

"It's okay. Forget I suggested it," Allie said.

Oops, she'd forgotten Allie was waiting for an answer.

"We'll stick to meeting in Putney on Sunday like we said. Anyone who's been to Curtis's wouldn't believe it if you gave up a chance to eat there, for some burgers on the grill."

She couldn't believe how much Allie seemed to care about her feelings and whether or not she was comfortable in a situation. The sincerity of Allie's response shot through an opening in Geena's tightly knit persona and went straight to her core. She didn't care if it was too early or not too early, but the thought of watching Allie cook burgers at some farmhouse in Vermont made it the only place she wanted to be.

CHAPTER FIFTEEN

"Y ou're as jumpy as cold water on a hot frying pan. I'm leaving. I'm leaving." Barb grabbed her keys from the hook by the side door.

"Thanks, Barb. I kind of feel like I'm kicking you out of your own house."

"No. It's fine. You keep wanting me to go into town more anyhow. And Jean and I wanted to see that matinee in Mortonsville. I promise you won't see my face until after suppertime. You're okay with feeding the critters?"

"No problem. Look at me—my hands are all shaky." She held them out and watched them tremble.

"You're not using any knives this afternoon, are you?" Allie shook her head and Barb took her hands. "I know you really like her, and this means a lot to you. You'll be fine—just be yourself."

"That's what they all say." She looked at Barb and squeezed her hands. "I don't want to fall into my usual trap of making this more than it is. But I see a different side of her on the phone than what she shows the rest of the world."

Barb squeezed back and leaned in close. "You keep on remembering that. And go slow. Okay?"

"That's why I wanted it to be only me and her today at

the farm. I don't want it to look like I'm introducing her to the family or anything. That would definitely freak her out."

"Do you want me to give you a call before I come home? This is the first time you've brought anyone to the house... and..."

"No, this is your house. We'll eat a late lunch, I'll feed the animals, and then I'm going to show her the Wellness Center, and she'll go back to camp."

"Good enough. I'll see you later."

Allie watched Barb leave, and then the house phone rang.

"I think I'm about fifteen minutes from you, but my GPS led me down a dirt road, and then I came out on a paved road, but I have no idea where I am, and I don't think I want to trust the GPS again. I know I'm a little early—I hope you don't mind."

Geena sounded a little nervous, and that made Allie smile.

"That's okay. Do you have a pen and some paper? I'll give you directions, or I could drive out and meet you if you tell me where you are. It can be a little tricky finding Town Farm Road depending which way you're coming into town. Where are you?"

"I have no idea. I'm pulled into a sort of farm stand–slash– gas station–slash–greenhouse place. The sign says *Windmill Farm*. I asked them, and they could get me to your town, but they didn't know the road."

"I know where you are. Ready?" Her heart beat faster knowing Geena was only fifteen minutes from her house. Fifteen minutes from her. Knowing Barb was coming home later would help keep her from moving too fast again.

"Ready. I wish your cell phone worked at your house, 'cause I'd send you a selfie of my big smiling face. I can't wait to see you."

"I can't wait to see you either, so let me give you the directions because I'm done with phone calls this week. I want to talk with you across the table from me." She wanted to do much more than talking, and her body seemed to know that Geena was only a few miles away. She rattled off the directions to the main road into town. "Got that?"

"Got it."

"That road will take you into Proctor's Falls. You'll see a little post office on your right, then a store. You'll come to a stop sign, and you want to turn left onto Carter Hill Road. Follow that for about two miles, and Town Farm Road will be on your left as well. We're the fourth house on the right. White with green trim."

"Like our little cottage."

Allie could almost feel Geena smile. She smiled.

"Like our cottage. Only much bigger."

"See you soon," Geena said.

"I'll watch for you."

❖

Geena turned left onto Town Farm Road. She drove slowly on the gravel road and counted houses as she passed them. Then she saw Allie stand up on the front porch of a small farmhouse and wave to her. She smiled and thought she would love to drive home and see Allie waiting for her every night.

"Geena!" Allie pointed. "The ditch!"

She'd been looking at Allie and not where she was driving, and her car had drifted to the right. She snapped back to attention, spun the wheel to the left, avoided the ditch, and pulled into the driveway all in one motion. She braked and rolled down her window.

"Ta-dah!"

"Nice save. Now follow the driveway around back. I'll meet you out there."

She drove around the farmhouse and parked the car. Allie was on the back deck. She took a bag from the back seat and brought it to her.

"What have you got in there?"

"I brought watermelon. I figured if we weren't going to get messy eating at the barbecue place, we could get messy eating watermelon. I actually don't know what I was thinking—it seems kind of silly right now." She felt like an idiot. Who brought someone watermelon? Her brain felt like mush lately. She had trouble staying on track with the kids at camp too. Her mind would wander, and she'd catch herself thinking about Allie or about something she said.

Allie took the bag from her and put it on the table. Then she held out her arms. Her eyes looked happy.

"Watermelon is perfect. I've missed you."

She walked into Allie's arms and held her. It felt so good to hold her. She didn't realize her back had been so tense until the tension dissolved when they held each other.

"Kiss me." Allie turned her face to meet hers.

She touched her lips gently to Allie's and kissed her with a tenderness she didn't know she had. Allie responded with an equal tenderness that made her knees go rubbery. She held on a little tighter, and Allie seemed to know what she needed.

"I might need to sit down." She felt a little light-headed too, but that might have been because she skipped breakfast in her rush to get to Vermont.

"Sure," Allie said, looking concerned. "Are you okay?"

"You knock a woman off her feet, that's all." She beamed a Geena smile, but Allie didn't look like she believed her.

"Not buying that. Although"—she sat down next to her—"that was an incredible kiss."

"It was. Did you feel that thing?"

"I did." Allie put her hand on Geena's arm.

"Really, I feel okay now. I skipped breakfast, and I think the combo of no food and that kiss did knock me off my feet."

"Let me get you something to drink, and the burgers are all set to go. I turned the grill on right after you called. I had a feeling you'd be hungry."

Geena leaned back in her seat and looked at Allie.

"I've never been this hungry in my entire life."

She watched Allie blush before she turned to go into the house, and Geena thought she'd never seen someone look so adorable and sexy at the same time. Without Allie to draw her gaze like a magnet, she looked out past the deck to a large barn and a fenced field. There were two small flower gardens encircled with fieldstones, and what looked like a small vegetable garden out to the left of the yard. There was also an old-time umbrella-like clothesline stuck into the ground near the back far corner of the house.

She liked the little town she'd driven through on her way to Allie's. She wondered what her cousin Barb was like. Allie had told her that Barb wouldn't be here today, and she had to admit she was relieved. She'd been to women's houses and apartments before, but not often, and never for lunch or dinner, and she always left before breakfast. Allie distracted her from any discomfort she had.

Allie came out the screen door carrying a glass of ice water and a plate of burger patties.

"Here's your water, and here's something to tide you over till the burgers are cooked." She pulled a granola bar out of her pocket and set the plate on the table.

"Thanks. That's perfect." She unwrapped it and took a bite.

"How do you like your burger? And I haven't shown you the house or where the bathroom is or anything. I'm so happy you're here, but I don't do things like this, having women over. Not because I don't like to—I've just never had the opportunity since I've been in Vermont, and before that, well, I told you how I took care of my parents for a few years."

"That's okay. Sitting was a good idea. And I used the bathroom at that farm stand place, so I'm all set for now." How much did she want to reveal? Well, she was here, wasn't she? "You know, I don't do this either, Allie."

"I find that a little hard to believe. I'm sorry, but I've seen a lot of photos of you."

"I don't do *this*. I don't have dinner with a woman at her house."

"Technically, it's not my house." Allie flipped a burger onto the grill.

"I don't have dinner with women at their relatives' houses either. And make mine medium." She didn't know how to let Allie know how different this was for her and how far out of her usual comfort zone. The funny thing was, she didn't feel as uncomfortable as she thought she might. She felt fine. Especially now that she had eaten the granola bar.

Allie flipped a couple more burgers on the grill.

"I'm making some for Barb to have later."

She could watch Allie flip burgers all day. Everything about her was perfect.

❖

Allie channeled her inner Mashley Whiplash and handled the grill like she used it every day. She didn't like grills—they had always intimidated her. Barb did all the grilling and her father had before that. She'd never owned a grill. But she'd been watching Barb the last few times she grilled and asked her a few questions. Now she took the buns and the burgers off the grill and placed them on plates with only a hint of grill-doubt.

"Grab your plate and follow me. I left all the fixings in the house." She opened the door for Geena, who put an arm around her waist and gave her a quick kiss.

"I couldn't resist. I find you quite irresistible."

The way Geena looked at her made her want to forget her plate of food and run with her up to her bedroom.

"I hope you find the food just as irresistible. I made a salad and picked up a peach pie for dessert. If you keep looking at me like that, I don't know what I'm going to do."

"Okay, I'll stop. For now. I don't want all this wonderful food you've made to go to waste." Geena scooped salad onto her plate and fixed her burger. "Are we eating in here or out on the deck? Hey, this is a beautiful house. I can see why you don't want to leave."

"It's not that I don't want to leave. Barb has needed the help, and it made sense to keep saving money until…" She didn't want to finish the sentence honestly.

"Until…?"

"Until the time was right to move out and the right… place came along." She didn't want to say *the right woman.* "I thought we'd eat on the deck."

"Okay, to the deck we go." Geena opened the door for her.

She watched while Geena bit into her burger.

"It's fabulous," she said.

Allie bit into her own burger. "It is pretty good." She was so relieved that her grilling came out all right. "Can I ask you something?"

"Sure you can. This salad is pretty tasty too. What's in the dressing?"

"I made it with cranberry juice because I didn't have any lemons. This week, when we talked on the phone, I loved hearing you talk about the theater camp and why you love it and love the kids so much. I was wondering, why did that one girl remind you of you when you were younger? Did you go to theater camp? Did they have it back then?"

Geena's face changed. The openness was gone. She put down her burger and wiped her face with her napkin. Then she balled up the napkin and held it in one hand. Tightly. "You've told me about your parents and how hard it was to take care of your father after he treated your mother badly all those years. I can't imagine that. It seems so easy for you to talk about your family. It's hard for me to talk about mine."

"Thanks. You're such a good listener. You say all the right things." She put her food down and reached across the small table to hold Geena's hand. "If you'd like to tell me about why that girl reminds you of you, I'm a good listener too." She hoped Geena knew she could tell her anything.

Geena took a deep breath, then said, "We talked one parents' day when no one showed up for her. She told me they probably forgot. *They forget lots of things that have to do with me,* she said. I told her I knew what that felt like."

Allie gently squeezed Geena's hand, to encourage her to continue.

"My parents were pretty old when I was born. I have two sisters who are thirteen and fifteen years older than me. As soon as I started elementary school, they were put in charge of me so Mom and Dad could have their lives. They were very busy people at work and socially."

"That must have been so difficult," Allie said.

"The four of them were a unit. I was the extra. Not really

needed for anything. But in junior high I found my tribe. I had a choice of taking art or drama, and I took drama. I built a different kind of family in my theater groups and camp. A family of choice—many families, really." Geena smiled, but then the smile died on her face. "My parents are *uncomfortable*, as they put it, with my chosen field of work. They never said anything after I came out. They didn't care. It didn't affect their lives. But seeing me in commercials and on the internet…they hated that. I made it public. What would their friends think, after all."

She put her other hand over Geena's hand and pulled her chair closer to her. Geena seemed to like that. She knew Geena well enough to know that she didn't share this information with most people. The last thing she wanted to do was make a misstep.

"I'm so sorry that happened to you. And I'm so sorry that's the way your parents treat you."

Geena looked down at their hands. "They were pretty much absent from my life. My sisters were supposed to take care of me. Well, supposed to isn't exactly what happened. Now that I'm older, I can see how unfair it was to them as well. But we don't have much of a relationship. They sort of went their way after college and I went mine."

Allie wondered if Geena had ever told anyone about this. The pain on her face was heart wrenching.

"That must have been so lonely and so hard. Did you have anyone you could talk to?"

"My best friend's mom was very nice to me, and I talked to her a few times. And I had my theater crew. A couple of teachers in school probably saved my life. Teachers don't get enough credit for what they do for kids like me. And a couple of great therapists when I was younger." Geena shook her head and gave a weak laugh. "I didn't think this was the way the afternoon was going to go. Wow, that was a lot. You're so easy to talk with. I feel so comfortable around you, Allie. Thank you for listening."

"I feel the same way. And you're welcome. Thank you for trusting me with your story." She kept trying to tell herself that she was reading too much into things, but she felt the same as Geena did. She was so comfortable talking to her that she felt like she could tell her anything.

Geena smiled a Geena smile, full of innuendo. "I wanted to tell you something else. Can we bring our plates inside? The sun is on my back and I'm getting hot. Or, you know, it could be that I'm in such hot company too."

Allie took both of their plates, and Geena took the drinks into the house where they settled in the living room. She put the plates on the carved coffee table.

"This table is wild," Geena said, admiring the piece.

"A friend of Barb's is a chainsaw artist, and he carved it for her."

"I love how the two gnomes on each end are holding up the main table. I've never seen anything like it."

"Barb tries to support local artists. Feel better? It's cooler in this room." She picked up her burger and took a bite. It was cold, but she didn't mind.

"There really is something else I wanted to tell you. It's been bugging me all week since we were at our cottage."

"I like when you say *our* cottage. It sounds so sexy."

"Did I?" Geena took a deep breath and blew it out, then looked out toward the kitchen. "I didn't even realize I did that."

"You did it before on the phone too. I liked it."

"Whatever happens between us going forward, I didn't want you to think that you did anything wrong at that cottage when we were in bed."

"You weren't feeling well. I understand." She still felt like it wasn't the whole story. Maybe Geena was going to tell her the rest of whatever was going on.

"I *wasn't* feeling well, but that wasn't all of it."

Allie put down her burger and turned to face Geena who didn't turn but stayed looking out at the kitchen or maybe just into space. She had no idea what Geena was going to tell her.

She watched Geena's knee bounce.

Allie tried to understand what strength it must be taking for Geena to expose herself this way. She sounded like she'd lived much of her life trying to protect her tender places from harm.

❖

"It doesn't feel right to keep things from you, and this has been bugging me. It's embarrassing, though."

"If you don't feel comfortable telling me, maybe now isn't the right time. And that's okay."

"I had our night at the cottage all planned. It's what I do. I love doing that, choreographing how the date is going to go and making it all go according to my plan. Then after you kissed me like you did, I had trouble thinking about what I was supposed to do next. On top of that, I started not feeling well, and I got angry at myself because things weren't going the way I wanted them to. Then I didn't care about the plan. I liked it when you were taking care of me."

She couldn't believe she told Allie about her family and all that stuff about what she was feeling at the cottage. She wasn't sure how Allie would react. She turned and looked at Allie's face and waited for her response. "Does any of all that make any sense?"

"It makes perfect sense that you would feel like that about your family. I'm so sorry about how hard it must have been for you. And I'm not happy you felt sick, but I'm happy your plan didn't go through. I liked talking with you at the cottage. Thank you for feeling like you could talk to me about this."

"I didn't disappoint you?"

Allie took Geena's hands in hers.

"No, not at all. I was confused because I didn't know what was going on, and it felt like you weren't telling me what was going on."

She had gone back and forth about telling Allie her side of the story about what happened at the cottage last week. She knew she could have kept up with her story of not feeling well after dinner, and Allie would have continued to believe her. Because that's the way Allie was. She didn't want to use Allie or tell her a lie. Truth mattered to her. Allie mattered to her, and that both excited and scared her at the same time.

"You're something else, Allison McDonald. Let's do something normal like finish our burgers. I'm sorry, everything's probably cold by now."

"And that's why they make microwaves." Allie picked up their plates and headed into the kitchen. She turned and looked over her shoulder. "Thank you for telling me what was really going through your head at the cottage."

"Thanks for listening. How about you show me the horses after we eat?"

"Sure. I'll need to feed them soon anyway."

❖

The house phone rang, and Allie answered it. It was Barb, warning her that she was on her way home. She was super apologetic, but Allie assured her it was no problem at all.

"Really, it's okay. I wanted to show Geena the Wellness

Center anyway. I'll leave your burgers in the fridge." She hung up the phone and brought their plates into the living room.

Geena must have overheard her side of the conversation and was now eyeing her quizzically.

"That was Barb. Her friend decided to cut their night short, so she wanted to know if she could come home early. She's so respectful. It's her house, for Pete's sake." She took a bite of burger. "Oh, this is not good. Don't even take a bite."

Geena took a bite.

"It's not too bad."

Allie smiled watching Geena trying to pretend the burger wasn't like a thick piece of cardboard.

"It won't hurt my feelings if you don't eat that burger. I guess I'm more talented with the grill than the microwave."

"Okay, good." Geena put the burger down. "I'll be honest—I don't want our date to end so soon. Did I hear you say you wanted to show me the Wellness Center? I'd like that."

"I'd like that too." Part of her wanted Barb to meet Geena so she could see how nice she was and how beautiful she was and how great she was. But she had no idea what direction whatever this thing with Geena was going. She liked this side of Geena when she turned the volume low and became more thoughtful and less showstopperish. She liked both sides of her.

"It's only a few minutes into town," Allie explained. "But you know that—you just came through town." She turned to face Geena. "I still can't believe you're really here."

"I kind of can't believe I'm here either, and that all this has gone down today. But here I am sitting next to you on your couch."

"Technically it's Barb's couch."

"Well, thank you, Barb, for the couch that I get to sit on next to Allie and kiss her."

"You'll have to hold that kiss. We need to get our plates in the dishwasher and get out of here before Barb gets home. She'll be here in about twenty minutes." The entire time she was talking, Geena was watching her lips move. For some reason her body was counting this as foreplay and responded.

"Can I kiss you when we get to the Wellness Center? Your mouth is wanting a kiss—I can feel it."

The desire she kept reining in and reining in made her a little light-headed. She couldn't ever remember feeling this turned on by a woman's gaze or her words. And the more she got to know Geena, the deeper the desire grew.

She nodded, grabbed their plates once more, and headed for the kitchen.

CHAPTER SIXTEEN

A llie unlocked the door to the Center and punched in the security code. Geena followed her into the building. She showed Geena the office and the session rooms on one side of the building, then brought her to the opposite side where her rooms were. She rented two rooms and used one as an office and a place to store extra supplies. Her rooms were the last two on the right. She opened the door to her office.

"And this is my office. I didn't want to invade Barb's house with an office, and it works much better having it here." She felt like she was sneaking around, but she came here a lot of times after hours and on the weekends to get paperwork done or work on advertising and social media promotions. Her hands were sweaty, and she could feel her heartbeat. She turned to get to the other door, and Geena was inches from her.

"And where do you see clients?" Geena ran her hands down the outside of her arms and held her hands, then leaned in and whispered in her ear, "Show me."

The touch of lips on her ear made her catch her breath. She stepped aside and opened the door to her massage room.

"In here." The steady undercurrent of desire punctuated her sentence.

She heard Geena close the door behind her. She turned to face her.

"Geena." Her voice came out an octave lower than normal. Her desire pulsed through every part of her body. When she first met Geena, her physical desire was confusing. Geena looked exactly like the woman she'd been phone dating. The woman who used Geena's photo to catfish her.

But after spending time with Geena, her desire multiplied as she got to know more about this beautiful, smart, funny, complicated woman.

"Allie, can I kiss you?"

"Wait a sec." She picked up a small remote from the countertop at the back of the room, and automatic blinds darkened the space.

"Do you mind if I lock the door?" She locked it with one hand, slipped her other arm around Geena's waist, and drew her close.

Geena's warm lips met hers, and each touch of Geena's tongue magnified her desire. Geena's hands moved under her shirt, and she murmured her pleasure. She took off her shirt and her bra, and Geena's hands followed the exposed skin as she drew the shirt over her head. Geena caressed her breasts with such a gentle touch, and she arched her back trying to push her breasts deeper into Geena's touch.

"You look better than I remembered. Now, let's get you naked," Geena said as she tried to unbutton her shorts.

"Let's get you naked too." She tucked her fingers into the waistband of Geena's shorts and unbuttoned and unzipped them. She knelt and pulled Geena's shorts down a few inches to kiss her hips, then her thighs. She slid the shorts down another few inches and paused at her knees. She caressed the backs of Geena's thighs while she kissed her knees, then slid the shorts down to the floor.

She could hear Geena's breathing grow more uneven and ragged, and she helped her step out of her shorts and her underwear. She moved her hands up Geena's calves, the backs of her knees, and the backs of her thighs, while she kissed and played the tip of her tongue over Geena's skin. Her own breath came fast and her hands trembled. The small part of her brain that was still able to think didn't want to come on too fast and strong.

Geena took her hands and motioned for her to stand up, then backed her against the door. Geena ripped her own shirt off and put her hands on either side of Allie's shoulders. She wasn't wearing a bra. She pressed the length of her body to Allie's and kissed her in a way that made clear that there was no too fast or too strong. Allie's body arched toward Geena's, and she wrapped her arms around her.

"Let me get my shorts off." She swooped her shorts and underwear off in one motion and tossed them. She smoothed her hands down Geena's back and over her rear and pulled her hips toward hers as Geena's tongue explored her neck and shoulder.

"You're so beautiful," Geena said between kisses, "and I don't think my legs will hold me much longer."

"Let me help you onto my table." She said the words in between setting soft kisses along her collarbone, then took Geena by the hand and led her to the massage table.

❖

Geena loved that Allie was such a powerful lover. She was used to women who wanted her to make their fantasy come true, and this was different and exciting. Allie's touch was so bold and confident it made her weak in the knees. She thought that was something that only happened in romance novels, but her legs were so wobbly Allie had to wrap an arm around her waist and guide her in the dark to the table.

"Come up here with me." She ran her finger along Allie's back as she put a small pillow under her head. She heard her fussing with something behind the table.

"In a minute. How about I relax you a little more." Allie's voice was soft and low, her smile playful, as she leaned over to kiss her. As their lips met, she heard a small noise, and one of Allie's hands, slick with warm oil, ran over her left breast and then her right in a slow figure eight motion.

She drew in a breath and felt her nipples tighten.

"But I want to touch you too. Come up here." She reached for Allie, who leaned over the table and ran both oiled hands down the outside and up the inside of Geena's thighs. Her legs parted, and Allie continued to use long, light strokes up and down her thighs. Her hands traveled up to her hips and back down again. Each long slow stroke both relaxed and excited her. Her mind relaxed, but her breath quickened. She tried to caress Allie as her naked body brushed over hers with each stroke.

"I'll be up there with you soon."

Allie kissed her, and then her hands had more warm oil and she continued the figure eight pattern around her breasts, but this time Allie circled closer and closer to her nipples. Her hips jerked involuntarily. This was one of the sexiest things that had ever happened to her. She felt like her body was under Allie's control, and she liked it. A lot.

"That's so beautiful. You're so beautiful," Allie said.

She loved hearing those words when she was in bed with a woman, but when they came out of Allie's mouth, something hard inside her broke and felt wonderful.

Allie's lips were on her nipple, and her tongue circled and circled, while her other hand stroked her left breast and slowly slid down her side. Geena opened her eyes, and for a second the thought crossed her mind to move Allie's hand. Allie's hand touched the outside of her breast, then slid down her rib cage to her hip and back up again, while her mouth kissed her other breast. Allie moved her lips right next to her ear. She couldn't believe she felt like she was going to come already.

"You feel so good," Allie said. "I'm going to move to the end of the table for a minute. I want to feel how wet you are. I think you might be very wet."

Geena made a sound when Allie said the word *wet*, and her hips jerked again when Allie's hand and mouth left her body.

"Stay here." She reached for Allie and found her breasts. She rolled each nipple with her thumbs, then reached down and found Allie. She groaned and thought she was going to come right then. Allie moved away from her, and her body felt vulnerable for a split second, but then she felt Allie's warm hands on her ankles. Allie spread her legs gently and ran her hands up the inside of her legs, then over her thighs and to her hips.

"Move down the table—I'll help you," Allie said.

She bent her legs and helped move her hips down the table toward Allie. She grabbed at the sheet and her back arched.

"I can't...wait...any...more." Geena grunted the words between breaths.

Then Allie's fingers were inside her and she came. She turned her head from side to side to try to keep from crying out.

"You're so beautiful. You are incredible. You feel so—"

Allie stilled her hand, then began moving her fingers in and out of her slowly. Every time she moved her fingers out of her, they circled, then stroked her clit a couple of times.

She reached down, took Allie's wrist, and placed Allie's hand on her thigh, then shifted onto her side. "I want you. Now."

Allie climbed on the table and lay beside her. She draped one leg over her hip as an invitation. "I'm yours."

"You might know your way around this table, but I think one of us is going to fall off. That's not how I want to end this day." She moved Allie's leg and slid off the massage table. She ran her hands over Allie's breasts, down her belly, to her thighs. Allie opened her legs.

❖

Allie'd already had several small orgasms while touching Geena. Right now, Geena's mouth and hands and fingers seemed to be everywhere on her, kissing her, stroking her, rubbing her. Her desire for Geena and Geena's desire for her was amplified by each kiss and every touch. She moved her hand between her legs. Geena gently moved it away.

"Now you move down the table for me."

She could hardly hear her request. She scooted down the table. She would do almost anything right now that Geena asked her to do.

"Bend your knees." Geena's voice came from the end of the table.

She bent her knees and felt Geena's hands sliding down the outsides of her thighs and under her butt, and felt her lay kisses on the inside of her right thigh. Something like words came out of her mouth. Then Geena's mouth was on her, exploring every bit of her, inside and outside, again and again. She grabbed behind her own knees and arched her neck and she came. Geena let up while she rode each wave that traveled up her body and back down to her center and up again.

Geena kept one hand on the inside of her thigh and moved until she was standing next to her face, then kissed her.

"I don't think you're quite finished." Geena stood back up.

"I'm fantastic. Unbelievably fantastic." She put her hands up to Geena's face and gently pulled her down and kissed her forehead and cheek, then her lips.

Geena took her hands and kissed each of them.

"What it is...?" she said, as she started to move away.

Geena's fingers traced a line down the length of her body, and she shivered in anticipation.

"What is it?" she asked.

"It's that I'm not finished with you."

And Geena's mouth was on her again.

She was about to tell Geena it was okay—she was indeed finished and that was okay. Because after a big orgasm, nothing aroused her. Her body told her it was satisfied. But as she started to talk, Geena's tongue made long, slow motions inside and outside of her. Her hips loosened and her legs fell open wider. A deep pressure grew inside her, and she bore down against Geena. Her hips made a grinding motion and she wanted more. More of whatever Geena was doing to her. She felt fingers inside her and Geena's tongue moved to her clit. She panted and mumbled something. Her hands twisted the sheet beneath her while Geena kept the slow pace.

The pressure she felt grew, and her hips pumped wildly, trying to make Geena move faster.

"More. Faster." The words flew out of her mouth.

Geena gave her what she asked for, and a tingling sensation moved up her legs.

"Slow..." She reached blindly for Geena's hand.

Then she felt like her whole body orgasmed as she bore down on Geena's hand again. A small rush of liquid ran out of her and onto Geena's hand. She'd never experienced anything like that. Ever. Her muscles relaxed, and Geena removed her hand slowly. As she did, Allie felt little pulses of tiny aftershock orgasms.

"Wow," Geena said.

"I've *never*…"

"No. Never?"

"No. Wow. I can't talk. My body is still—"

"Easy, baby. Let me get up there with you and hold you. My legs are all wobbly again. I think I came when you did."

Geena climbed onto the table and stretched out alongside her. She wrapped one arm around her back. Her face was about an inch from hers.

"You're incredible," Allie said. "What'd you do to me?" She had no words to describe what she felt.

"You're the incredible one. Everything we did felt so easy. You feel so beautiful. When I touch you, it's like I know what you like already. When you touched me, I…I don't know…it was different in an amazing way."

"Me too." She kissed Geena and the aftershocks started again.

Geena held on to her, wrapped a leg over her hip, and took Allie's hand and put it between her legs.

Geena whispered, "Touch me once and I'm there."

"No falling."

"No falling."

She felt Geena's wetness with her fingers and slowly eased into her. And out. And in again. Geena turned her face into the small pillow, cried out, and hung on to her, then kissed her for a very long time.

Allie stopped kissing and picked her head up. "Did you hear something? Something running?"

"Only your heartbeat, baby. Come back."

"I definitely hear something." She removed Geena's leg from her side, sat up, and carefully got off the table. She didn't know who would be here making noise. No one usually worked on Sundays. If someone was and they saw Allie's door closed, they wouldn't disturb her.

"Kind of chilly without you here."

"Shh." She reached under the table. "Here's a blanket."

Allie found the remote and opened the blinds an inch. She went to the door, turned the lock, and opened it a crack. She clearly heard a vacuum cleaner. She closed the door and locked it again.

"The cleaners are here. Oh God, I hope they didn't hear anything. We need to get dressed. I don't want them to think I have a client in here."

Geena wrapped the blanket around her and sat up.

"But isn't that what you do in here? You have a person on the table, naked?"

"But I'm not usually naked, silly. And we look like we've had sex."

"You definitely look like you've had sex." Geena smiled. "And I definitely feel like I had sex."

❖

Geena thought Allie looked so adorable standing by the door with her hands on her hips, even though the room was darkened. It had been so long since she'd experienced the give and take of making love, when she'd been so young and inexperienced back in college. But right now, in this room with Allie, she felt free, like anything was possible. She felt like she didn't need to play a role with Allie.

Her clothes landed in her lap. Allie'd started getting dressed.

"Could you come here for a minute?" She held out her hand to Allie.

"Sweetie, we really need to get dressed."

"I know. I'll get dressed in a minute." She started lowering the blanket over her breasts. She looked at Allie while she lowered the blanket.

Allie stepped closer.

She continued to lower the blanket.

Allie started to kiss her chest, talking to her in between the kisses that now moved down to her breasts.

"Your skin tastes so good. And I noticed you like it when I kiss you here, and here."

Allie kissed the outside of her breast.

"I do."

Allie kissed tiny, barely there kisses along her rib cage.

"That feels good."

"You seem to like a lot of things I do."

"Especially trapeze. When I saw you on that trapeze and at your game…"

"You looked sexy on the trapeze too."

She felt Allie's kisses move to her stomach. Allie kissed her way back up to her breasts, then her neck, jawline, and lips.

Geena took a deep breath. She felt like she'd been holding her breath for years.

Allie put her hands on her face and held it while she looked into her eyes.

"You are the most beautiful woman I've ever met. And I don't mean only on the outside. I'd love to stay here for about twenty-four hours kissing you, but we need to get dressed."

Geena felt her eyes fill. She was so used to pushing aside her vulnerable self and behaving like Geena the sexy player would, so she could hear women tell her she was beautiful, and sexy, and hot, and pretty, and stunning, and all those things women said to her and she needed to hear to feel okay. And she needed to hear it over and over again to feel even somewhat okay. If one woman said she was beautiful, would the next woman? Her relationship with women was all about getting them into bed and into a place where they said she was the best, the most beautiful, the sexiest. It was never enough. She could never hear those words enough.

She heard Allie say she was beautiful, and she felt beautiful for the very first time in her life.

CHAPTER SEVENTEEN

Allie peeked her head out of the door of the massage room. "I don't hear anything. The rug looks freshly vacuumed. I think they're gone." They were both dressed and ready to leave.

"Do you think they were right outside the door and we didn't hear them?" Geena came up behind Allie and wrapped her arms around her.

"I think they were. They must have thought I was working in here because there was only my car in the parking lot. I didn't hear them try the door, did you?"

"I didn't hear anything but you talking to me. Now that we know they're gone, maybe we should stay." She put her hands on Allie's hips, then played with the zipper on her shorts.

"We just got everything all cleaned up and set for my clients tomorrow. Plus, as wonderful as this was, I want to be next to you, or on the same bed as you, next time." She removed Geena's hands and turned around to face her.

"Next time could be right around the corner," Geena said. "I'm sure there's someplace we could go. It's not that late." She pulled her phone out of her pocket. There was a message from her agent, but she ignored it. "It's still early."

She tried to give Allie a convincing kiss.

"All of a sudden, I'm hungry." Allie patted her belly.

"Me too." She hooked a finger in one of Allie's belt loops and pulled at it.

"I mean *food* hungry. There's no place in town that's open, but we could go across the river and get pizza or a sub or something. Let's get some food and we can talk about how horny...I mean hungry you are."

"Only if we can talk about how hungry you are too. You were *really* hungry a little while ago. In ways I could have only dreamed about." She ran her fingers down Allie's arm and took her hand and kissed it.

"Now that I've unleashed you, what am I going to do?" Allie asked.

"I think maybe I should be the one asking that question." She'd imagined how Allie would be in bed, and her imagination hadn't come close to the reality. She knew Allie was a physical person, between her job and the derby, but she wasn't prepared for this woman who was so comfortable with her body and with Geena's body. Her confidence in her sexuality was intoxicating. She wanted more. As soon as possible.

"You come with me to get some dinner, and I'll find a place for you to stay tonight, and maybe I won't go back to the farm tonight." Allie moved her hips closer to Geena's.

"I'll have to think of ways to turn that maybe into a yes." All she wanted to do was turn that maybe into a yes.

"You'll have to convince me while we're out in public eating dinner."

Allie turned and walked down the hallway, and she followed. Once they were in the car, she remembered the message from her agent and how sketchy cell service seemed to be up here in this part of Vermont.

"Do you mind if I check my phone? I think I might have a message from my agent. She knows I'm at camp, or supposed to be at camp, so it must be important."

"Sure, go ahead. I'll call Barb and tell her I'm going to be late."

She saw there were two messages from her agent. She opened them, read them twice—a production company really wanted to meet her—then sent her reply, while she heard Allie's voice in the background as she talked to Barb. She put her phone to sleep and stuck it in her back pocket. While Allie said good-bye to Barb, she looked out the window at the big Victorian house. The sign *Harvest Hill Wellness Center* had smaller signs below it, each hanging by two hooks. One sign read *Allison McDonald, LMT*. She thought it was a pretty little town with the all the small businesses surrounding the green.

Her agent's message swung her mind back to her life in Boston. She thought about how Allie might be able to get away to Boston every now and then, and their summer fling could continue after camp ended. She liked that idea.

"I told Barb I'd be late, and I wasn't sure yet how late." Allie's hand rested on her thigh. She smiled at Geena. "Was your message important? Sorry, none of my business, really."

"No, it's okay. Good news for my career maybe. One of the biggest streaming services in LA is interested in talking to me about a series they're doing. My agent's going to find out more and get back to me." This was the next step in her career. To be in LA. She tried not to think ahead—most times these things didn't pan out. There was always lots of talk, though. Thankfully she had a great agent and she filtered most of the chatter.

She thought she saw a flicker of disappointment in Allie's face before she replied.

"That's great. This could be your big break, right? When does camp end, anyway?"

"Two weeks."

"Two weeks? Really? I mean, I know it's a summer camp,

but I guess I thought it went through the whole summer until Labor Day or the end of August. I didn't realize it ended so soon." Allie took her hand away and placed it on the steering wheel.

"When we first met there wasn't any reason to tell you, then things changed at the cottage, and now…" Geena looked out the passenger window and took a deep breath. What was happening? She felt closer to Allie than to some people she had known for years.

"I guess we both got caught up in this thing we have between us."

"Chemistry—"

"Electricity." She and Allie spoke at the same time. There was something between them, she knew that. But she felt like she didn't know much more. A hundred thoughts piled on top of each other in her head. Along with a hundred questions. She didn't want to figure any of this out. This was why she always liked things simple. You played, you had a great time, you moved on. But this was different. Part of her didn't feel like moving on. A big part of her.

Allie laughed and shook her head. She had the most fabulous laugh.

"I think we should talk about this thing we have. But I'm starving. Is it okay with you if we go get some food?"

"Can we eat in your car? I don't want to talk about anything in a room full of people, and I don't want anyone to recognize me." She only wanted to be with Allie. She was sure they could figure something out. She'd never thought to tell Allie when camp ended. She didn't plan for any of this.

Allie backed up the car and pulled out of the parking lot and onto the road. "How about you order while I drive, and then I'll go in and pick it up?"

"Perfect."

❖

Allie stood in line to pick up their subs and fought the lump in her throat and the feeling that she might cry. She'd gone into this with her eyes wide open. She'd researched Geena on the internet—she knew the score before they met. Plus Geena had told her to her face that she didn't do relationships. She knew this was going to be a summer fling and that was it. But she hadn't counted on Geena showing her the woman behind her public persona. She hadn't counted on what happened at the cottage and what they revealed to each other during all those long phone calls this week. And she certainly couldn't have predicted what just happened at the Wellness Center.

But Geena should have told her that her time at camp was almost over. She felt angry about that but didn't want to spoil their night or what little time they had. She'd promised herself she wouldn't move too fast, and here she was again. Her heart knew that Geena was her person. The one you waited for. The one you hoped you'd find when you were alone in bed, late at night, thinking about your life.

She knew she was more than a fun night of sex to Geena. But she didn't know what she was. She wanted to find out.

When she walked out of the diner, Geena ran around the car and opened the driver's side door for her, then took the drinks tray from her and went back around the passenger side.

Allie turned each sub over in her hands and read the writing on them. "Roast beef for you and pastrami for me. Here's some napkins." She unwrapped her sub and bit into it. "This is the best thing I've tasted."

Geena looked at her and smiled. "I don't think mine is going to be as good."

"Roast beef, right? I got the right one?"

"It won't be the best thing I've tasted today."

Allie felt heat flood her face. "I'm glad we're not in the sub place, because I know my face is red." She thought back to the massage room and what it felt like to have Geena's mouth on her. She knew Geena was trying to make light of the fact that she didn't tell her when camp ended.

"It is. You look adorable."

She didn't want Geena to keep playing and flirting to avoid their conversation. She was going to be as honest as she could with Geena. After she took another bite of her sub.

"I wish you'd told me that camp ended in two weeks." She was angry about that. It seemed like a deception.

"What difference would that have made? Would you have canceled on me?" Geena wiped her mouth with her paper napkin and took a sip of her drink.

"No, I wouldn't have canceled, but I would have known how much time we had. You knew how much time we had."

"I didn't know how this was going to go, Allie. And I live in Boston, not Tokyo. We could still see each other if we decided to do that."

"It sounds like you've already had this conversation with yourself, but not with me. And now there's California." She thought if she'd known Geena was only at camp for two more weeks, maybe she wouldn't have seen her, maybe she would have called Charlie. Maybe she wouldn't be sitting here thinking that she'd met her once-in-a-lifetime person. Her throat felt tight and she didn't want to cry.

"I have to be honest with you. All of this is new territory for me. And it's happened so fast. It's not like me. I'm Geena and I've been acting like…"

"Acting like what?"

"Virginia. That's the name on my birth certificate. Virginia Harris. My family called me Ginnie, and my mother's family is Italian, so Geena wasn't a big stretch. I'm Ginnie when I go home. But everywhere else, I'm Geena. Except with you. You seemed to see past that, right from the beginning when I first met you at that coffee place. I tried to shrug it off at first, but you were so sincere. That was one of things that was like a magnet—instant attraction. I couldn't stop thinking about you, even when I knew I should." Geena pulled her hair back away from her face.

Allie said, "I saw some article that mentioned your birth name, but you never brought it up, so I figured if you wanted to, you would. I thought it fit you, when I first saw it. You might not believe this, but when I think of you, I think of you as both Virginia and Geena. Maybe because I have my derby persona, Mashley, I can understand a little. I'm all Mashley when I'm skating, but in my regular life I'm mostly Allie, with a smattering of Mashley. She's always been part of me, but the derby gave that part of me a name."

"Geena would never do what I'm doing. But I don't think it's like your derby name. I don't show the part of me that's Virginia to *anyone* anymore. Ever. But with you, everything is different."

"So what do we call what we're doing? Are we dating? What happens when you go back to Boston and to California?" Her heart pounded as she asked the questions. It was hard to swallow her bite of sub. She washed it down with her drink.

"There's a good chance I won't ever hear about the California thing again. Lots of jobs get funneled to my agent. She tells me about the ones that have some promise, but most of them don't happen. If you want to be an actor, you have to have nerves of steel, and a good agent."

Geena touched her face, made eye contact. "We've managed to see each other under odd circumstances. I'm at camp and only have one night off a week, and you live in a place with no cell service or internet. I think we've done pretty well. I like getting to know you. I think we have fun together, don't we?"

"Fun. Yes, we have fun." First Geena told her that she felt like herself when she was with her, and then it was like she flipped a switch and said they had fun, like it didn't really mean anything. Allie wrapped up the rest of her sub. She didn't feel hungry anymore. "I remember you said all you wanted was a little fun for the summer."

Allie thought she could almost literally see the soft part of Geena shrink back and disappear while Geena the actress took over. Maybe if this was the dance, she thought, she didn't want to be involved.

"We still have two weeks. I'll be busy with the end of the summer plays, but I'll still have some time off. My cabinmate Melissa even said she'd cover for me. We still have time to get together a couple of times, maybe. We can still have a lot of fun." Geena finished the last bite of her sub and rolled the paper up into a ball. "Give me yours—I'll stick them in the bag."

"I'll take it." Allie scrambled out of the car before Geena could see she had tears in her eyes. She walked slowly to the trash barrel so she could get herself together. They did have two weeks left, and Geena didn't say they couldn't see each other after she left camp. But she felt like she was doing it again, making more out of a relationship than the other person wanted. She was almost ready to go along with the two weeks of fun that Geena wanted, but she caught herself.

"I thought this night was going to end a very different way."

"It still can, you know," Geena said. "We're here. There's probably a hotel or B and B nearby." Geena reached over and stroked her cheek. "You've had some food, but I would bet you're still hungry." Geena came closer and kissed her cheek, then her lips.

She turned to meet Geena's lips. Kissing women was always wonderful, but kissing this particular woman went beyond anything she had ever experienced. What she felt when they kissed was different than two people merely having fun. She knew it, her body knew it, and her heart knew it.

"I didn't expect to like you so much," Allie admitted. She put her hands on Geena's cheeks and looked into her eyes.

"I don't see that as a problem." Geena smiled and gave Allie a quick kiss.

"I wish I could say that I'm totally okay with having more fun for the next couple of weeks, but I don't know if I am."

Geena sat back in her seat and looked out the passenger window.

"So this was a one-time deal for you."

"No, I'm not saying that." She knew she was trying to protect herself. What would be so bad about going to bed with Geena again tonight? That was the problem. Nothing about it would be bad. It would probably flood her heart with so many feelings, and the woman next to her would just be having fun. She didn't like how that made her feel. She guessed she wasn't a fling type of person after all.

She turned to face Allie again. "What *are* you saying?"

"I'm saying that I've spent a lot of time going along with whatever women want from me, to please them. Even if it's not what I want. And I promised myself I wasn't going to do that anymore. And yes, I thought...I *hoped* we would end up in bed somewhere along the line today. And I thought I'd see you again. But when you got your message and told me when camp ended, it rattled me. My body would love to go to a room with you tonight and continue where we left off, but the rest of me is saying *Wait a minute*."

"I'm sorry if I upset you. I don't think you're a one-time deal either. Wait, maybe that came out wrong. I mean, I don't know what's going to happen when I get back to Boston or out in California, but I want to keep seeing you after camp is over. I'm sorry I didn't tell you camp ended in two weeks. I think I wanted to stay in the space we created for ourselves and didn't want to think about real life."

"Thanks, but this is my real life. I'm not in some fantasy world. I live here, and I work here. I invited you to my home. This is me. I didn't realize I was indulging someone's fantasy." She pictured all those photographs online of all those women who had dated Geena. Maybe she was totally wrong about everything and she was only Geena's next fling after all.

❖

That last line hit Geena like a brick wall. That was exactly what she did with the women who claimed to love her and wanted to have sex with her. She indulged their fantasies. And she knew how she felt afterward. Like it didn't really matter who she was, if she played the part they wanted her to play. She didn't want Allie to feel like that, ever. She had been acting like this wasn't Allie's real life. It was true—she didn't want to think about her real life when she was with Allie, because everything was so unlike her real life when she was with her. Everything felt more real than her life as Geena on *Days and Nights*, where she was Hot Geena who would have sex with any woman, any time. She turned and held out her hands. Allie took them in hers.

"You're right. This is your real life. Thank you for inviting me up here." She had no idea what to say next.

She thought maybe she was wrong to pursue this thing with Allie, whatever it was. But she couldn't remember a woman ever affecting her this way. Her head told her to leave Allie alone, but she felt so comfortable with her and liked being with her so much. And the sex wasn't just sex. When they were in Allie's massage room, she forgot who she was supposed to be, and nothing existed except her and Allie. She had no idea what would happen after camp ended and she went back to Boston, but she knew she didn't want to hurt Allie or disappoint her. She hadn't been thinking of Allie, though. She'd been so caught up in how *she* was feeling that she'd never stopped to think how she was invading Allie's real life.

"Why don't you take me back to my car, and I'll drive back to camp. I don't want this night to end, but I'm not going to push you. I don't want you to go all Mashley on me." She tried to lighten the tone of things. Not successfully, by the look on Allie's face. "Can I still call you at our time this week?" Geena felt overwhelmed by all the emotions churning inside her. She felt like she was in completely new territory, and there was no GPS.

"Yes." Allie kissed her on the cheek. "Yes, you can."

CHAPTER EIGHTEEN

After Allie had watched Geena take the right turn out of the driveway last night, she'd sat on the front porch and gone over their night together. She knew who Geena was and what she wanted when she went into this, so it wasn't like Geena tricked her or lied to her. Each time they saw each other or talked on the phone only confirmed what Allie's heart was trying to tell her. She was in love with Geena, and what she felt was different from other times with other women.

As she drove to work she kept processing what had happened. Last night at the farm and later in her massage room had felt nothing like any date she had experienced. Their time together felt like a benediction, like something pure and sacred passed between them. It was much more than sex. She had been sure Geena felt it too, but then later, not so sure. She parked her car in the Wellness Center's parking lot. She was glad it was a short day, because she wasn't sure how she would get through the day without thinking about Geena and what happened in her massage room last night.

Part of her wished she could go home right after work and call Geena, but she had practice tonight. The Green Mountain Mavens of Mayhem practiced a few nights every week throughout the summer but always tried to fit in one or two extra practices during the week of a match. So tonight, she'd get her Mashley on.

❖

She didn't talk to her teammates about her dates with Geena. She was afraid that Venus or Candy, Geena's superfans, would post something online about it. But that didn't stop them from asking questions.

"Mashley, did you ask Geena what her favorite foods are? I saw online that she likes burgers." Candy skated over to Allie as she laced up her skates.

"I couldn't tell you." Allie finished and stood up next to Candy. She wanted to get out on the track. She felt stronger and more confident out on the track than anywhere else.

Candy and Venus skated on either side of her as she made her way out of the locker room and onto the floor. Their practice space was in an arena that belonged to a private school in Barre. Candy and Venus stopped in the doorway, blocking Allie.

"You know. Why don't you want to tell us?" Venus put her hand on the doorway. "We know you went out with her after the match, and we saw you were at Barclay's Burgers."

"Were you there?" Allie put her hands on her hips.

"Leave Mashley alone, ladies."

Her teammate Red Hot Mama was behind her.

"Saw it on Facebook," Candy said. "You should be careful, Mashley. I don't think she's your speed. Just looking out for you."

Allie clenched her fists. She felt a pat on her butt from Red Hot.

"Don't let them bother you. Use it to play," Red Hot

whispered in her ear. "Step aside, ladies, coach is waiting for us."

Red Hot Mama skated out onto the arena to the area of the floor taped off in the shape of an oval. Mashley, Candy, and Venus followed her.

As Allie skated around the track, she thought about what Candy said. She crouched and used her thigh muscles to take her faster around the track. She wove in and around her teammates. On her next time around, she saw her four teammates in blockade form. They motioned for her to try to break through. She always had the advantage at practice of knowing her teammates' weaknesses. She aimed right for them and easily broke through and skated another lap hard and fast. She was different from the other women Geena had been with, she thought, only maybe not the way Candy meant. She loved her. She said it again to herself. She loved Geena. She loved Ginnie Harris. The coach's voice caught her attention as she skated by.

"That was fun, ladies, now let's do some drills."

She slowed down and met up with her teammates.

"What was that about?" Red Hot Mama asked.

"Are you pissed at us?" Venus linked arms with Candy.

Allie felt like her whole body was smiling.

"She sure as shit doesn't look pissed off," Red Hot said.

"Hey, Blue Girl." The coach pointed to a group of newbies who were interested in derby. "Let Mashley show you what the jammer does." The coach continued to match up newbies to Mavens of Mayhem skaters. Several times a summer they opened practice to women who were interested in skating. They taught them about the derby, did a few drills, and spent most of the time skating in the typical derby crouched position. That usually weeded out a bunch of hopefuls.

Allie spun around backward and forward as she skated around the track with Blue Girl, explaining the role of the jammer. She thought Blue Girl had great instincts—she would look ahead at the other skaters and weave around them as they continued to skate around.

"You look like you really love it." Blue Girl smiled at Allie.

"I'm loving everything today," Allie replied. She couldn't stop smiling.

❖

Geena finished supper and went into the restroom to see if Allie had tried to call or text. She knew she had practice tonight, but she hoped there might be a message anyway. She closed the stall door and checked her phone. Nothing from Allie, but there was a text from her agent.

Call me asap.

She sent her a text instead. *Do you really need me to call?*
Yes.

She pressed her agent's number on her phone and she picked up on the first ring.

"I've got good news and bad news."

"Hit me with the bad first." She leaned against the wall in the bathroom stall.

"*Days and Nights* is over."

"They canceled my show?" Geena thought she must have misheard her.

"Not canceled exactly. One of the producers got into some financial trouble and shut everything down. Somebody might pick it up, but your best bet right now is California. They messaged me when they heard the news and reiterated how interested they were. They offered to pay your airfare."

"Well, that sucks." Her mind jumped from one future scenario to another. She thought she should feel more upset than she did. Maybe she was in shock or something, because she felt sort of relieved.

"We can fix this." Her agent talked fast. "You'll be okay. Now that they know your show here is gonzo, we might have a harder time negotiating your salary, though. You're done with that camp gig next weekend, right? They're paying to fly you out there next Sunday. You can drive from your camp to Logan and get your flight. You'll meet with them on Monday after you get in. Hey, I'm sorry about *Days and Nights*. And I know you're not supposed to be making calls. I'll message you after I book the flight. It's all good, Geena."

"Thanks. Sure. Sounds good." She couldn't quite believe *Days and Nights* was over. She'd miss her coworkers, of course, and everyone who worked on the show. She hung up the phone and started back to her cabin. She'd been so lucky to get acting jobs starting in college. She loved the attention she got, and when she first started in the business, she'd driven herself to work more and more until her name was known locally. She'd worked on branding herself so she could be the one in control of how others saw her. She'd focused all her energy on one goal: to hear over and over again that she was beautiful and desirable.

She never let any woman get close enough to hurt her. She'd stuck by her one woman, one date rule, although if the sex was good enough, the one date sometimes ran into two or three days. Getting that fix of attention and compliments was what drove her, and she became an expert at manipulating her feelings to justify whatever she did to get those compliments.

These past few weeks with Allie tossed everything on its head. She had no desire to pretend to be anyone else with Allie. The more she got to know Allie, the easier it was to share about herself. She picked up a piece of a dead pine branch and broke it into little pieces as she walked to her cabin. She didn't want to stop seeing Allie. And she wanted to make sure Allie knew that. She turned around and went back to hide in a bathroom stall one more time tonight.

CHAPTER NINETEEN

Allie came home from practice and dropped her gear bag. Barb was in the living room watching a movie.

"You're home early."

"Practice ended early. Can I talk to you when your movie's over?" She sat on the couch and bounced her knee.

Barb picked up the remote and turned off the DVD player.

"It looks like it's something that can't wait. Is it about last night? I didn't expect to see you here this morning. I thought it was going to be the big night." She looked at Allie and raised her eyebrows.

"It was." She felt her neck and face grow warm. "And today I realized—now don't say anything bad, okay?—I realized that I'm in love with her."

Barb looked at her but didn't say anything.

"I know what you're thinking. That I always move too fast, and then get hurt. But this is different. It really is. I can be myself with her. I'm not pretending to be whatever I think she wants. I'm completely me. I've never felt this way before with anyone."

The look on Barb's face told Allie she was skeptical at best.

"What happened to *love the one you're with* and *having a good time* and *getting some?*"

"I tried to do that, but it obviously didn't work. I had to tell someone else my news. It came over me tonight as I was skating around the track. I think she's my once-in-a-lifetime person, and not because I need her to be that. It just... happened."

"But didn't you say she wasn't into relationships and all that? She doesn't even live near here. I guess the most important question is, do you know how she feels?"

"No, like I said. I don't know how she feels, and I don't know what's going to happen. I don't have a plan. And isn't it great?" Allie got up from the couch and leaned over to give Barb a hug. "I can't wait to tell her."

"You're gonna tell this playgirl that you're in love with her?"

"In my gut I think she knows there's something special between us. She's a little afraid of that." Allie had never felt this way before. She hadn't molded herself to what she thought Geena wanted or expected—she was only being herself. Her only wrinkle of doubt was she wasn't sure what Geena would say or do when she told her.

"Oh, Allie. I don't want to see you get hurt again. You said you were going to have a summer fling and not get caught up in things." Barb stood up and hugged her. "I love you. You're one of the most decent people I've ever known. You put too much trust in people sometimes."

She hugged Barb back, then stepped away.

"That's okay. I don't ever want to be afraid of living my life anymore. My life, not the life someone else wants. I sent her a text when I left practice and asked if she might be able to talk tonight at nine. I'll eat something, and then I'm headed into town to check if there's a text from her."

"I'm here for you. No matter what."

"I know. I've always known that. Thanks. You can finish

your movie. Are there leftovers?" She felt so lucky to be living with Barb. If she lived alone, she'd be bouncing off the walls wanting to talk about Geena. Barb was so grounded. Maybe a little too grounded tonight, but she always put things in perspective for her because she knew her so well.

"Always."

"I love you, Barb. I don't tell you often enough."

"You've always been my girl, Allie." Barb quickly brushed a knuckle against the corner of her eye and looked away. "Go make yourself some food now." She waved a hand in the direction of the kitchen.

Allie made and ate a chicken salad wrap, then headed into town. She parked at the library and took out her phone. She saw a message from one minute ago from Geena.

I miss you. I know you're at practice, but I'd love to talk to you tonight. I'll wait here for a while in case you're still in town and get this message.

She texted back immediately.

I'm here! Call me.

Her phone vibrated. "I'm here."

"So you are," Geena said. "How was practice?"

"Practice was wonderful. I'd like to tell you about it in person." She could hear her heartbeat as she thought about telling Geena that she was in love with her.

"Really? Because I wanted to talk to you about something too, but not over the phone."

Allie's heart sang. She thought it would be so romantic if they both discovered they were in love with each other on the same day. They'd talk about it when they were older and told people how they met and fell in love.

"This is crunch week at camp with the final two plays and saying good-byes to some of the kids. I don't think I could change days off with anyone or drive up there. Sorry."

"What if I drove down? You have a curfew, right, but you could go out after dinner?"

"I might be able to arrange that. There's a convenience store about half a mile from camp. I'll text directions. Are you sure you don't mind driving down here? I wouldn't be able to meet you until about eight o'clock, the same time we call. That's when I'm usually free."

"I can't wait to see you. Tomorrow night?"

"Me either. Eight o'clock tomorrow night."

Allie drove home with the radio turned up and the windows rolled down. She sang along with the radio even though she didn't know the words and couldn't remember ever feeling so happy.

❖

Geena fidgeted in her bunk all night long, replaying their short phone conversation and trying to read more into what Allie said. Why didn't she ask Allie more questions when she had her on the phone? All she knew was that Allie's skating practice was wonderful, and she wanted to see her. That must mean she wanted to continue to see her, even after camp, even if it meant sporadically. But maybe it didn't mean that at all. Maybe Allie's practice was wonderful, and it reminded her that she'd had a wonderful life before she met Geena. She knew Allie well enough to know that she wouldn't say good-bye over the phone. She would want to do it in person.

These thoughts bounced around in her mind all day long and through dinner and a mini-rehearsal after dinner. Her anxiety grew as the time to meet Allie got closer. She rushed back to her cabin after dinner to change her clothes and get her car keys. Melissa was already in the cabin reading a book.

"Why are you changing?" Melissa put her book down.

"I'm meeting Allie at the store. I'm going to tell her about California. She has something she wants to tell me too, but I can't figure out what it is. I'm not sure when I'll be back, so don't wait up. I've got to get going."

She didn't want to be late for her meeting with Allie. She grabbed her keys and headed to the door. She half ran down the path to the parking lot, got in her car, and tried not to toss gravel as she turned onto the main road. Allie didn't sound upset on the phone, but that didn't mean she wasn't. Geena played out as many scenarios as her mind would let her in the four minutes it took to get to the convenience store. Allie was waiting in her car.

She parked and waved Allie over to her car.

It was difficult for her to believe they had seen each other the night before last. It seemed longer. She watched Allie walk to her car, and her body tensed in anticipation. She rubbed her palms on the front of her pants. She didn't know if Allie had good news for her or bad news. It took forever for Allie to get to her car, and she couldn't take her eyes off her.

Geena had never understood what people were talking about when they said *She glowed* or *Her face glowed*. Now she knew.

Allie opened the car door and got in and turned to face Geena.

"We do a lot of talking in cars, don't we?"

Everything Geena had wanted to say slipped away for a minute as she looked at Allie, speechless.

"Is everything okay at camp?"

Geena leaned across the console and kissed her. Kissing Allie was so easy and sexy and new every time they kissed. It was like they discovered new things about each other every time they touched.

"I've missed you. I think you are more beautiful every

time I see you, but especially tonight. Everything's fine at camp. How are you?"

"I'm so happy. I made this discovery during practice yesterday and it was incredible." She leaned toward Geena again. "I know that camp is going to end very soon."

"I'm so sorry I didn't tell you that."

"I know, that's not it. I didn't want any more time to go by before you knew. Before I told you." Allie laughed nervously. "This was so easy last night, lying in bed rehearsing it."

"That can happen with rehearsals. Sometimes when it's the real thing you have to ad-lib a line or two."

"I think that's what I'm trying to tell you." Allie took one of her hands in hers and looked into her eyes. "I think this *is* the real thing. What we have. What's going on between us."

This wasn't what she'd expected. She definitely liked what was going on between them, but she wasn't ready to define it.

Geena said, "Well, it's definitely powerful and not like anything I've experienced. The other night was unbelievable. I hope this means we can get to know each other even better than we did in your massage room." She smiled, hoping she'd lightened Allie's mood a little, but a pinprick of fear touched her heart. Allie looked very serious.

"Geena...Ginnie Harris..." Allie kissed the back of her hand. "I've fallen in love with you. I love you. And I couldn't wait any longer to tell you."

Panic gripped her heart and a band of fear tightened around her chest. Other women had claimed to be in love with her or said she was their soul mate or other half. But they didn't know her—they only knew Geena from *Days and Nights* and what they saw on the internet. She never let anyone come closer than that. Except Allie. Everything she had planned to say to Allie disappeared, and there was only a blank space filled with fear.

"I don't know what to say." She felt like her words were coming out of her mouth very slowly. Her hands started to sweat.

Allie spoke very softly. "You could tell me how you feel about me."

She took her hand away from Allie and wiped her palms on her pants again. She blew out a breath. "I…I don't know."

"Why did you want to see me? I thought you wanted to talk about us?"

"I did. Sort of. I had another message from my agent. The next season of *Days and Nights* is on hold, indefinitely. The producer has some money trouble. Which means I have no job. I had to make a quick decision and decided to go to California and audition for that part. My agent thinks she can get me more jobs out there, especially now that I'm free. I'm leaving as soon as camp ends next week."

"I'm sorry about your show. Oh, Geena, this is your dream, isn't it." Allie's fingers touched her upper arm. "To be in LA and work on a big production. You must be so excited."

"I am. It's been a dream for so long and now it might come true." She knew she needed to say something about Allie's soul baring. "About us. We can still see each other when I'm in town. And you could fly out there sometimes. I know I like to be with you." She liked Allie a lot, and she was so relaxed and comfortable with her. But her declaration of love hit her hard and scared her.

"You know that would be difficult for me. I have a business to run and can't fly back and forth from California. But I don't regret anything. I want you to know that. I don't regret telling you that I love you. Because I want you to know. You weren't just a summer fling for me." Her voice wavered. "I tried hard to make you a summer fling, but you crept in here." She pointed to her chest, and then she took Geena's face in her hands. "I know you'll do great in California or wherever you go." She smiled. "I want you to have your dream. I really do." Allie took her hands away and looked out the passenger window.

"Allie...I..."

Allie turned back to face her. She didn't say anything but looked into her eyes, then leaned over and kissed her on her cheek.

"Yes." Allie's face was inches from hers.

The urge to kiss her and hold her was so strong, she tucked one hand under her thigh. She knew Allie wanted words right now, not kisses, but she had no idea what to say. It was so easy to disengage herself from other women and their feelings, but not from Allie.

"I think you're amazing." She didn't know what to say, and that sounded so inadequate. She had no line for this occasion.

Allie pulled away. "I think you're pretty amazing too. I've got to get going." She opened the car door. "Let me know about the job."

She watched Allie get out of the car, shut the door, walk to her car, and leave. Her heart thumped in her ears as she watched Allie drive away. She drove back to camp and sat in the parking lot crying and trying to figure out why.

❖

Allie drove home in a silent car, up the dark interstate to Proctor's Falls. She'd been so happy on the ride down and so sure of her feelings and Geena's feelings. She hadn't expected Geena to offer a declaration of love necessarily, but she could have said something about their special connection. Allie knew they had one, like she knew she had two hands.

But after Geena told her the news about California, and she saw the happiness and excitement on her face, she knew she couldn't get in the way of her dream. She loved Geena and she wanted her to have all her dreams. When she drove through town, she wondered if Geena had sent her a message after she left. She had to check her phone before she headed back home to Barb's. She pulled into the Wellness Center parking lot and looked, but there were no messages.

She knew she wouldn't be going out to California, and once Geena got busy, she probably wouldn't be coming back east either. Allie knew how important dreams were. Hers kept her going through a lot of difficult stuff. But she still felt gut punched. She'd thought Geena was in love with her too. But all Geena said was that she was amazing. She couldn't believe she had misread someone again and so completely.

As she drove to the farm, she turned the air-conditioning off and opened her windows. She wanted to smell the mountain air she loved so much. Geena had said she wanted to get to know her better, and they'd shared so much about their lives over the phone and when they were together. Allie knew she wasn't pulling Geena into something or making up how close they had become. Their night together wasn't a dream. The past few weeks weren't a dream. She knew Geena shared what she'd felt. She knew that was true down to the core of herself. And if Geena did get the California job and they had to say good-bye, at least they'd both know how the other felt. Allie missed her already.

She pulled into the driveway of the farm and realized that despite her disappointment, there were good things that had come out of this. This time was different than her other relationships. She didn't chase after Geena, and she didn't try to make herself over to become what Geena wanted. She had been enough. Being herself somehow had the power to help Geena relax and drop her sexy star power act. She'd had the courage to be herself with another woman, and it felt good.

Barb had left the back deck lights on for her like she always did, but when she looked at the deck, she saw her and Geena, laughing and making burgers. She turned off the ignition, went up the deck steps, and sat in the chair Geena had sat in. She put her head in her hands and cried. She felt her heart breaking apart.

CHAPTER TWENTY

With the staging of four final productions, the last two weekends at camp were full of promises to keep in touch and good-byes for staff and campers. All four plays were wonderful, but Geena thought her kids' production of *Victoria Martin: Math Team Queen* was the most fun and got the biggest round of applause. By the end of camp, she was always anxious to get back to her life in Boston, but this year she wanted to get as far away from the East Coast as possible. She couldn't wait to get on her flight to California.

After her big cry the night Allie drove away, she tried to put the past couple of weeks behind an internal door, where she kept other tender things, and got on with being Geena. She changed the time she checked her phone back to the morning after breakfast and resisted the urge to wait in the restroom at eight every night in case Allie called. There was no reason for her to call, and she didn't. There were never any messages or texts from Allie when she checked in the morning. She thought about texting her but didn't know what to say.

She was packing up the last of her things into a large duffel bag when Melissa came in the cabin door.

"You're really going to California?" Melissa put her hands on her hips.

"This could be my dream job. When a big production

company wants you to audition, you go audition." She sounded much more confident than she felt. Once she left camp and got back to acting, she'd feel more like herself.

"You know, I'm probably butting in where I shouldn't." Melissa walked in front of Geena to catch her eye. "I know how much you like her, and I know it probably scares the shit out of you."

"Hey, I like her a lot. And yeah, you're butting in, but that's what friends do. Allie wants me to go to California. She knows this is my dream. She respects that. That's the way she is." She reminded herself that she didn't get attached to women. Allie knew that from the start.

Melissa held up her hands in front of her. "Got it."

"I don't want to miss my flight. I'm cutting it close already. Love you." She hugged Melissa. "See you after I get back."

"Let me know how it goes."

Geena lifted her bag and headed out the door, and she waved over her shoulder. "Yup."

She drove to Boston and met her agent in Newton to get a suitcase full of clothes. Her agent had packed a bunch of her makeup too, and good thing, because a glimpse in the rearview mirror told her she needed the strong stuff. She continued on to Logan Airport and her flight to California. She moved through the security checkpoints in the airport and stood in line with her boarding pass.

She felt lucky to have this opportunity. She knew so many actors who would be jealous right now. She knew this was the right thing to do. Allie was a nice person and she never wanted her to think she was leading her on. Her summer at camp and her time with Allie were such a great escape from her real life.

"Geena!"

She heard her name and turned. Two young women held cell phones pointed at her.

"Are you Geena? Can we get a selfie?"

This was her life. This was what she wanted. She wanted women to want her. To want a selfie with her, to want to go to bed with her, to want to interview her, then feel her up in the hallway afterward and tell their friends they touched Geena. She posed, then handed her boarding pass to the gate agent at the counter and got on the plane.

She put her small bag in the overhead compartment and felt her phone vibrate. She excused herself to the woman beneath the compartment, dug the phone out, and sat down.

Is camp over? When can we get together again?

When she first glanced at the message, she thought it was Allie and her heart quickened. Then she saw it wasn't Allie's number and a second text came.

Saylor

Oh. The hippie girl from the Cape. They'd had sex a few times before she left for camp. She figured Saylor would keep texting if she didn't answer her.

On my way to California on business, on plane now, will talk later.

Sure, Saylor replied.

A few minutes after the plane took off, a young woman asked the man sitting next to her if he'd like to switch seats with her and pointed toward the front of the plane. He got up and took his new seat up front, and she sat down. She whispered, "I won't give you away. I'm one of your biggest fans, and I can't believe we're on the same plane together. You are Geena, right?"

"Yes. Nice to meet you." It still surprised her sometimes how many people recognized her. She held out her hand. This was going to be a long flight.

"I've watched all the episodes of *Days and Nights* at least three times each. My friends and I have a blog where we write about the show. I can't believe I'm sitting here next to you. I'm trying to keep it together because I feel like screaming right now. My name is Carrie."

"I hope you won't scream." Geena yawned. "I'm a little tired." She didn't want to talk with Carrie. She was hoping to use this time to figure out plans for whether or not she got the job on the new series. She knew she'd go back and say good-bye in person to her parents and a couple of her castmates from *Days and Nights*. This job could be really big. She wished she felt excited about it, but she only felt sad and fidgety. She'd been all caught up in camp ending, and helping to close up until next summer. Then she'd rushed to meet her agent and get this flight. This was the first time in days she could just sit with nothing to do and nowhere to be. She felt achy, like she was coming down with something.

"You look tired. Do you need anything? Should I ask for a drink or something? You're still so beautiful in person even if you're tired. I bet everyone who meets you wants a picture with you, right? I won't do that. I respect your privacy."

Sure, you do, she thought. *That's why you're jammerin' away at me.*

"Thanks. I'm all set."

It was a long flight and it looked like she was stuck with her biggest fan, so she could at least have fun with it. Carrie was older than her usual fans. Attractive in a perky sort of way. Maybe she needed a little fan attention. She'd been at camp all summer and away from her life. She needed to get back to herself again. She turned in her seat as much as she could to face Carrie.

She looked Carrie up and down. "You can't be traveling alone?" She glanced up front. "Is someone up there wondering why they're sitting next to some random guy?" She smiled her Geena smile.

"No, I'm alone. I mean, I'm going to visit my aunt in LA. I'm not with anybody. I mean, I'm single."

Carrie seemed a little flustered. It was Geena's job to fluster her some more. She was out of practice.

She leaned a little toward Carrie and lowered her voice. "I can't believe someone as charming and pretty as you is single."

Carrie's cheeks grew red, and she twirled her long hair with her finger.

"And I can't believe that Geena is asking me if I'm single. You're amazing. I have goose bumps sitting next to you. I follow all your social media and the *Days and Nights* website. This is like a dream."

"Show me those goose bumps. You're so cute." She knew all the right words to say to reel Carrie in, but she was having trouble getting back into character completely. Her mind kept wandering back to her first meeting with Allie at the coffee shop in Brattleboro.

Carrie held her forearm up to show her, and Geena traced a finger from her wrist to her elbow.

"You're easily excitable, then." Geena smiled.

She could see Carrie's chest rise and fall as her breathing quickened, and she watched her shift in her seat.

"Geena, I...are you...Oh my God, I can't believe I'm sitting here and you're talking to me about...about..." Carrie rubbed the palms of her hands on her bare thighs. "Things like this don't happen to me in real life. I don't have to go straight to my aunt's house. I would give anything to, you know, be with you. I wouldn't tell anyone either, like some of those women do online. Not me. I'm not like that."

As Carrie talked, the words *real life* rang in Geena's ears. Carrie had a real life. Allie had a real life. But she didn't. This wasn't a real life—nothing about it was real. Everything she said to Carrie was acting. She always loved the playing the

LANEY WEBBER

seducer and hearing women tell her how beautiful she was. Or she used to. Before she went away to camp. Before she met Allie. The sadness she felt earlier welled up again and caught in her throat.

"Of course you're not. You seem like such a nice person."

Geena thought Carrie looked confused for a moment.

"Thanks."

"I'm sorry, I'm more tired than I thought. I think I'm going to try to take a nap."

"Oh, sure, sure. Do you need a pillow or anything?" Carrie asked, unable to mask her disappointment.

"I'm fine." She turned away from Carrie and shut her eyes. The sadness she felt earlier welled up and caught in her throat. She missed Allie. A cry almost escaped from her as she realized what it would mean to no longer have Allie in her life. She wanted to be with Allie and do all the things they were doing. She wanted to make plans with Allie, no one else. When she thought about her future, she and Allie were cooking burgers and laughing. In her mind she saw Allie kissing her tenderly.

That was real life.

She breathed in a deep breath and let her heart feel what it had been denied for so long. Connection and love. She opened her eyes. She loved Allie. Oh my God, she thought. She loved Allie. And she knew Allie was in love with her.

An urge sprang up out of nowhere to tell Carrie and tell the whole plane and get the pilot to turn the plane around. Her life was waiting for her, and she knew it now. She had the courage to let herself feel. She turned and looked at Carrie. No, on second thought, she couldn't tell anyone. It would be all over social media in minutes. Okay, she thought. She wasn't going to tell everybody.

❖

The meeting went better than expected. The producers were developing a series that would stream on one of the most popular streaming channels. It was an ensemble cast, and she read for the part of the sexy lesbian attorney. She started reading the scene with a young man. He stopped her and told her to try it with a Boston accent. Her damn Boston accent that she'd spent years trying to get rid of. She almost laughed.

"Can you give me a minute?" She thought his name was Brad, but she wasn't sure.

"Okay," the young man said.

They offered her the part practically before she finished her take. She went through with the meeting because it didn't look good to cancel or not show up, but she knew she couldn't take the part. She didn't want to live on the other side of the country from Allie, and she knew Allie wouldn't leave Vermont. Allie had told her it was her dream life. And so she would have to hope someone picked up *Days and Nights* and they started production again, or her agent found her something closer to Allie. Because that's where she wanted to be.

A young man asked her to come into another room where another man and a woman were seated at a table. They introduced themselves, but the only name Geena could remember was the woman's name, Bellamy something.

Geena said, "Thank you for asking me to come out here to audition. This sounds like a fantastic project. Unfortunately, I'm not able to accept at this time." Her palms were sweaty. She put her hands in her lap and tried to inconspicuously wipe them on her pants, so she'd be ready for handshakes. She didn't like to refuse work, especially a project that appeared made for her, but her life wasn't going to be work anymore. She knew she'd figure it out.

The three people on the other side of the table looked at each other, and Bellamy spoke first.

"We're so disappointed to hear that. We watched the audition and think you're our perfect Gisela. What if I call your agent again? Is there something special you need?"

Geena couldn't believe how much they seemed to want her. Things like this never happened. What the heck, she'd be honest. She had nothing to lose, right?

"Thank you again. It's not that I need anything special. But I met someone recently, and it's serious, and she lives on the East Coast." She couldn't help but smile thinking of Allie. "It's bad timing for my career, I know—"

"Oh, Geena. That's wonderful news. But we thought you knew. Production for this project is based in New York."

"In New York?" She couldn't believe it. She didn't want them to take the offer off the table. She'd seen stranger things happen, so she spoke quickly. "That makes all the difference. You have my agent's contact information. I'm very interested, and thank you very much. The project sounds fantastic."

All three of them stood at once. Bellamy extended her hand.

"Wonderful news. We'll be in touch." She handed Geena a business card. "If you'd like to stay in town for a day or two, call this number and ask for True. She'll book a hotel and your flight home and assist you with whatever else you might need."

She put the card in her pocket, shook hands with the two men, and left. When she got to the lobby, she asked the receptionist for the carry-on bag she'd brought from the hotel, and then she went into the lobby café and called the number on the business card.

"True here."

"Hi there, my name is Geena and I—"

"Bellamy told me you'd be calling. I have a choice of two hotels for you. One closer to some clubs and the other closer to the airport. Which would you like?"

"Thanks, but I don't think I'll be staying. Can you get me on the next flight out of LA back to Boston?"

CHAPTER TWENTY-ONE

Each day at the Wellness Center, Allie tried not to look at her phone in between clients, at lunch time, and before she left for the day. She tried not to make special trips into town over the weekend to check her phone. Barb was trying to cheer her up by making her favorite foods. Her coworkers at the Wellness Center asked if she was okay on more than one occasion. They offered her acupuncture, Reiki, and reflexology. All her energy was focused on her clients. The intensity of how much she missed Geena surprised her. She was truly happy Geena was going for her dream, but her heart still ached knowing they wouldn't be together. She knew she couldn't make a long-distance relationship work, and she didn't want to try. Even with Geena.

It was just over two weeks since she'd met up with Geena at the convenience store and told her that she loved her. A couple of times, late at night, she thought that maybe she'd been foolish to tell her. But no matter what happened or where Geena went, Allie wanted her to know that she loved her. It was a chance she'd been willing to take.

She added a couple of appointments to her work schedule on her computer. Her desk phone rang. It was an internal call.

"Hi, Allie here."

"Rob and I want to know if you want to go out to lunch with us." It was Mary Ellen, the Center's owner. "We're only going across the street. You don't have any clients at lunch today, do you?"

"No. I think I'll stay in. But thanks."

"You've been staying in a lot. How about some sunshine? It's good for you."

"I've got work I have to catch up on. I'm okay." She looked at her too clean desk.

"Okay, maybe we can bring some sunshine back with us for you. We're leaving in five if you change your mind."

"Thanks for understanding, Mary Ellen."

She heard several of the practitioners leave for lunch and watched them walk across the street. She didn't want to go anywhere, because everywhere reminded her of Geena. Even though Geena only came to Proctor's Falls that one time, everywhere she'd visited seemed charged with vivid memories. She didn't know if she wanted the memories to go away or stay. She turned away from the window and back to her desk.

❖

True was able to get Geena on a red-eye from LA to Boston. It was supposed to get her to Boston by eight thirty a.m. Her plan was to drive to Vermont directly from the airport. She wanted her real life to begin as soon as possible. Her agent texted while she was at dinner and relayed details of the contract. Geena thought they must have sent it to her as soon as she left the building. This was going to be the best paying gig of her life.

She tried to sleep on the flight back to Boston, but her head was full of ideas about all the things she wanted to do with

Allie and what she would say to her when she saw her. She must have fallen asleep at some point, because the next thing she knew, she opened her eyes and it was daylight. She looked at her phone. They were about thirty minutes from Boston. After they landed, she found her car in the lot, typed *Proctor's Falls, Vermont* into her map app, and headed out. She was thrilled to be traveling north because all the commuter traffic headed south into Boston, and it was bumper-to-bumper.

The trip would take two hours and forty-one minutes, according to her phone. She figured it would feel like forever, but the opposite was true. The time flew as she pictured Allie at the farm and at her derby games. She couldn't believe how full her mind was of things she wanted to tell Allie and things she wanted to do with Allie.

Her phone told her to take the next exit. She didn't know how to get to the farm but knew the name of the Wellness Center where Allie worked. And so did her phone. She followed the directions, and when she looked up and saw the sign that read *Welcome to Proctor's Falls, A Nice Place to Live* her heart warmed. She thought so too.

She pulled into the parking lot of the Wellness Center and saw Allie's car. Her hands shook and her heart raced. She thought she might have trouble finding Allie, but she was here, and the reality of that hit her. For a second she wondered if Allie might be so hurt and so angry that she would turn her away. *You won't know the answer to that, Geena—no, Ginnie— until you go in there and see her.* She checked her face and hair in the rearview mirror one last time. It was difficult for her to know whether she was feeling excitement or anxiety. She took a couple of deep breaths and breathed out slowly like she taught the kids at camp when they were nervous.

She walked on wobbly legs across the parking lot and up the stairs to the Center. She opened the door. The waiting room was empty. No one was at the reception desk. She paced back and forth twice, then sat in a wood rocking chair. She figured Allie would have to come out of her office sometime. She rocked and waited.

❖

Allie finished the sandwich that Barb had made her and downed a few gulps of iced tea. Her next appointment wasn't until three o'clock, and she thought she might bring some sheets and towels over to the local laundromat. It was something to do. She opened the closet in her office and took out a mesh hamper. She found her keys in her backpack and pocketed her phone. She dragged the hamper into the hallway and shut her door behind her. The hamper was awkward to carry—she had to keep looking around the side of it to see where she was going.

"Can I help you with that?"

She looked in the direction of the voice and dropped the hamper. Sheets and towels were strewn at her feet.

"What are you doing here?" Her tears, which were right below the surface every day now, filled her eyes. She started to walk, and her feet got caught in a sheet. Geena caught her and held her.

"I wanted to surprise you."

"You did." She had no idea why Geena was here, and she didn't care.

Geena's arms felt so good around her. She'd thought she would never feel them again. She wrapped her arms around Geena.

"I see that." Allie sniffed into Geena's hair, and Geena held her tighter and said, "You're shaking. Are you okay?"

All she could do was nod.

"Don't cry." Geena put her hand gently on the back of Allie's head and said softly into her ear, "I wanted to tell you that I love you too."

"Aww," said a woman in the waiting room.

Allie had forgotten they were in the waiting room in the Wellness Center. She pulled away a little and searched Geena's face. She smiled so wide she thought her cheeks might crack. Geena smiled back.

"Come outside with me." Allie took Geena's hand and led her out the door and down the stairs. She walked her around the side of the building. "I love you," Allie said and stroked Geena's hair. "I'm so happy to see you. You didn't get the job?"

"I got the job, and I discovered my heart again, and you're the one who's in it."

Geena took Allie's hands in hers.

"The new series is set in Boston, and it's made in New York. One of the reasons they wanted me was for the accent. After all that work putting the letter *R* back into my words, they want me to take it out again." She laughed.

"You'll be in New York?" Allie couldn't believe it. They could do New York—it was only a few hours down the interstate. But she didn't know if Geena wanted what she wanted. She was in love with her and didn't think she could be in a casual relationship with her. "I have a million thoughts swirling in my head right now."

Geena brought Allie's hand to her lips and kissed the back of it. She looked up at Allie.

"Being here in Vermont with you and getting to know you helped me uncover the self I buried for so long, the self who was covered with layers of what I thought was sexy and desirable and lovable. I thought being desired and adored was the same as being loved. You showed me that it wasn't. You never required me to be the onscreen Geena. You gave me the freedom to be me, the me who was under all of that. I want to be with you, Allie. You were right, you know. What we have is the real thing."

"You want to be with me, like, in Vermont with me?" Allie's voice pitched higher than normal. She held Geena's hands and looked into her eyes.

"Like in Vermont with you, in Canada with you, in Peru with you. Anywhere you are, that's where I want to be. I can commute when I'm working in New York. The bonus is I love it up here. Not only because you are here, but because it reminds me of Western Mass where the theater camp is, and I've always been my most relaxed self there. That's a long answer, but yes, I want to be in Vermont with you and build a life together. I love you. I'll never get tired of saying that, ever."

Geena's words tumbled over each other in Allie's ears. The way Geena looked at her made her heart soar. She stepped closer and put her arms around Geena's waist. She loved Geena and Geena loved her. It was amazing. She couldn't remember ever feeling so happy.

"Kiss me." She moved closer and their lips met. She kept smiling while they were kissing. She felt Geena's lips move into a smile, but they didn't stop trying to kiss in between smiles.

As they were kissing, something large bumped against the back of Allie's legs, knocking her off balance. She grabbed Geena's arm.

"Elvis!" She disengaged herself from Geena's arms. "He's Buster's dog. He gets out and finds trouble."

The big yellow dog stopped and turned around as if to say, *What? I'm busy.*

Allie patted her pants pockets looking for something to

entice Elvis with while Geena started to walk toward Elvis, who curled his lip.

"Don't," Allie cautioned. "He'll only come if you have a treat."

Instead of running the other way, Elvis trotted toward Geena. She bent down, tucked one hand under his collar, and scratched him behind his ears with the other.

"I'm going to take off my belt. Can you help me?" Geena said.

"Now that's a great line." Allie kissed her on the cheek and unbuckled her belt.

They used Geena's belt as a makeshift lead. It looked like Elvis had fallen in love with Geena too. He leaned into her and looked up at her, panting with adoration.

"After we get a house, can we get a dog? I've always wanted a dog." Geena looked at Allie with a look very similar to the one Elvis was giving to Geena.

Allie took Geena's hand and kissed her on the cheek. She wanted to give her everything.

"I think it's going to be difficult to say no to you about anything. A dog? A house?"

"I meant it when I said I want to build a life with you. Here in Vermont. I'm crazy in love with you, Allie. Is it too much too fast? I guess I haven't even asked you if you want me here in Vermont. With you. And a house. And a dog. Elvis, sit." Elvis sat. Geena bit her bottom lip. She reached up and touched Allie's cheek. "Do you?"

"Yes, my love." Allie smiled. "Yes, to all of the above. I love you."

"I love you."

"Let's get Elvis back to Buster's store where he belongs. And then I'd like to take you somewhere and make love with you for about three days. But I have two clients this afternoon."

Allie wanted to cancel her clients and spend every minute with Geena but knew she couldn't do that to her clients. She had some money from her parents' house, but if they were going to buy a house, she needed to keep her business in good shape and maybe expand it. *Whoa, Allie.* Now she was getting ahead of herself.

"Reality just bounced back and hit us in the face," Geena said, flashing a wry smile.

"How does that feel?" Allie tentatively asked.

"I'm happy you have clients, and I'm happy I'm holding this silly dog with the silly lip. I'm happy that you're beside me. I'm happy I'll see you later, and tomorrow, and next week. My whole world looks and feels so different, knowing I love you and you love me."

"I know. Same here." She squeezed Geena's hand.

Geena held Allie's hand in one hand and Elvis's lead in the other and they walked together to Buster's store.

About the Author

Laney Webber has lived in four of the six New England states. Her love affair with reading and books began when she read the line "Sit, Spot, Sit!" in her first-grade class. Laney lives in Vermont with her wife; their rescue dog, Gracie; and their rescue cat, Rudy Valentino. She works as a librarian, which gives her free access to shelves and shelves of books. She believes that libraries are the best places to visit on the planet. When Laney doesn't have a book or pen in her hand, she likes to camp and wander around New England. Visit her website: www.laneywebber.com; friend her on Facebook @laneywebber.author; follow her on Twitter and Instagram @LaneyWebber.

Books Available From Bold Strokes Books

Face the Music by Ali Vali. Sweet music is the last thing that happens when Nashville music producer Mason Liner and daughter of country royalty Victoria Roddy are thrown together in an effort to save country star Sophie Roddy's career. (978-1-63555-532-5)

Flavor of the Month by Georgia Beers. What happens when baker Charlie and chef Emma realize their differing paths have led them right back to each other? (978-1-63555-616-2)

Mending Fences by Angie Williams. Rancher Bobbie Del Rey and veterinarian Grace Hammond are about to discover if heartbreaks of the past can ever truly be mended. (978-1-63555-708-4)

Silk and Leather: Lesbian Erotica with an Edge, edited by Victoria Villaseñor. This collection of stories by award-winning authors offers fantasies as soft as silk and tough as leather. The only question is: How far will you go to make your deepest desires come true? (978-1-63555-587-5)

The Last Place You Look by Aurora Rey. Dumped by her wife and looking for anything but love, Julia Pierce retreats to her hometown only to rediscover high school friend Taylor Winslow, who's secretly crushed on her for years. (978-1-63555-574-5)

The Mortician's Daughter by Nan Higgins. A singer on the verge of stardom discovers she must give up her dreams to live a life in service to ghosts. (978-1-63555-594-3)

The Real Thing by Laney Webber. When passion flares between actress Virginia Green and masseuse Allison McDonald, can they be sure it's the real thing? (978-1-63555-478-6)

What the Heart Remembers Most by M. Ullrich. For college sweethearts Jax Levine and Gretchen Mills, could an accident be the second chance neither knew they wanted? (978-1-63555-401-4)

White Horse Point by Andrews & Austin. Mystery writer Taylor James finds herself falling for the mysterious woman on White Horse Point who lives alone, protecting a secret she can't share about a murderer who walks among them. (978-1-63555-695-7)

Femme Tales by Anne Shade. Six women find themselves in their own real-life fairy tales when true love finds them in the most unexpected ways. (978-1-63555-657-5)

Jellicle Girl by Stevie Mikayne. One dark summer night, Beth and Jackie go out to the canoe dock. Two years later, Beth is still carrying the weight of what happened to Jackie. (978-1-63555-691-9)

My Date with a Wendigo by Genevieve McCluer. Elizabeth Rosseau finds her long-lost love and the secret community of fiends she's now a part of. (978-1-63555-679-7)

On the Run by Charlotte Greene. Even when they're cute blondes, it's stupid to pick up hitchhikers, especially when they've just broken out of prison, but doing so is about to change Gwen's life forever. (978-1-63555-682-7)

Perfect Timing by Dena Blake. The choice between love and family has never been so difficult, and Lynn's and Maggie's different visions of the future may end their romance before it's begun. (978-1-63555-466-3)

The Mail Order Bride by R. Kent. When a mail order bride is thrust on Austin, he must choose between the bride he never wanted or the dream he lives for. (978-1-63555-678-0)

Through Love's Eyes by C.A. Popovich. When fate reunites Brittany Yardin and Amy Jansons, can they move beyond the pain of their past to find love? (978-1-63555-629-2)

To the Moon and Back by Melissa Brayden. Film actress Carly Daniel thinks that stage work is boring and unexciting, but when she accepts a lead role in a new play, stage manager Lauren Prescott tests both her heart and her ability to share the limelight. (978-1-63555-618-6)

Tokyo Love by Diana Jean. When Kathleen Schmitt is given the opportunity to be on the cutting edge of AI technology, she never thought a failed robotic love companion would bring her closer to her neighbor, Yuriko Velucci, and finding love in unexpected places. (978-1-63555-681-0)

Brooklyn Summer by Maggie Cummings. When opposites attract, can a summer of passion and adventure lead to a lifetime of love? (978-1-63555-578-3)

City Kitty and Country Mouse by Alyssa Linn Palmer. Pulled in two different directions, can a city kitty and a country mouse fall in love and make it work? (978-1-63555-553-0)

Elimination by Jackie D. When a dangerous homegrown terrorist seeks refuge with the Russian mafia, the team will be put to the ultimate test. (978-1-63555-570-7)

In the Shadow of Darkness by Nicole Stiling. Angeline Vallencourt is a reluctant vampire who must decide what she wants more—obscurity, revenge, or the woman who makes her feel alive. (978-1-63555-624-7)

On Second Thought by C. Spencer. Madisen is falling hard for Rae. Even single life and co-parenting are beginning to click. At least, that is, until her ex-wife begins to have second thoughts. (978-1-63555-415-1)

Out of Practice by Carsen Taite. When attorney Abby Keane discovers the wedding blogger tormenting her client is the woman she had a passionate, anonymous vacation fling with, sparks and subpoenas fly. Legal Affairs: one law firm, three best friends, three chances to fall in love. (978-1-63555-359-8)

Providence by Leigh Hays. With every click of the shutter, photographer Rebekiah Kearns finds it harder and harder to keep Lindsey Blackwell in focus without getting too close. (978-1-63555-620-9)

Taking a Shot at Love by KC Richardson. When academic and athletic worlds collide, will English professor Celeste Bouchard and basketball coach Lisa Tobias ignore their attraction to achieve their professional goals? (978-1-63555-549-3)

Flight to the Horizon by Julie Tizard. Airline captain Kerri Sullivan and flight attendant Janine Case struggle to survive an emergency water landing and overcome dark secrets to give love a chance to fly. (978-1-63555-331-4)

In Helen's Hands by Nanisi Barrett D'Arnuk. As her mistress, Helen pushes Mickey to her sensual limits, delivering the pleasure only a BDSM lifestyle can provide her. (978-1-63555-639-1)

Jamis Bachman, Ghost Hunter by Jen Jensen. In Sage Creek, Utah, a poltergeist stirs to life and past secrets emerge. (978-1-63555-605-6)

Moon Shadow by Suzie Clarke. Add betrayal, season with survival, then serve revenge smokin' hot with a sharp knife. (978-1-63555-584-4)

Spellbound by Jean Copeland and Jackie D. When the supernatural worlds of good and evil face off, love might be what saves them all. (978-1-63555-564-6)

Temptation by Kris Bryant. Can experienced nanny Cassie Miller deny her growing attraction and keep her relationship with her boss professional? Or will they sidestep propriety and give in to temptation? (978-1-63555-508-0)

The Inheritance by Ali Vali. Family ties bring Tucker Delacroix and Willow Vernon together, but they could also tear them, and any chance they have at love, apart. (978-1-63555-303-1)

Thief of the Heart by MJ Williamz. Kit Hanson makes a living seducing rich women in casinos and relieving them of the expensive jewelry most won't even miss. But her streak ends when she meets beautiful FBI agent Savannah Brown. (978-1-63555-572-1)

Face Off by PJ Trebelhorn. Hockey player Savannah Wells rarely spends more than a night with any one woman, but when photographer Madison Scott buys the house next door, she's forced to rethink what she expects out of life. (978-1-63555-480-9)

Hot Ice by Aurora Rey, Elle Spencer, and Erin Zak. Can falling in love melt the hearts of the iciest ice queens? Join Aurora Rey, Elle Spencer, and Erin Zak to find out! A contemporary romance novella collection. (978-1-63555-513-4)

Line of Duty by VK Powell. Dr. Dylan Carlyle's professional and personal life is turned upside down when a tragic event at Fairview

Station pits her against ambitious, handsome police officer Finley Masters. ((978-1-63555-486-1)

London Undone by Nan Higgins. London Craft reinvents her life after reading a childhood letter to her future self and, in doing so, finds the love she truly wants. (978-1-63555-562-2)

Lunar Eclipse by Gun Brooke. Moon De Cruz lives alone on an uninhabited planet after being shipwrecked in space. Her life changes forever when Captain Beaux Lestarion's arrival threatens the planet and Moon's freedom. (978-1-63555-460-1)

One Small Step by MA Binfield. In this contemporary romance, Iris and Cam discover the meaning of taking chances and following your heart, even if it means getting hurt. (978-1-63555-596-7)

Shadows of a Dream by Nicole Disney. Rainn has the talent to take her rock band all the way, but falling in love is a powerful distraction, and her new girlfriend's meth addiction might just take them both down. 978-1-63555-598-1)

Someone to Love by Jenny Frame. When Davina Trent is given an unexpected family, can she let nanny Wendy Darling teach her to open her heart to the children and to Wendy? (978-1-63555-468-7)

Uncharted by Robyn Nyx. As Rayne Marcellus and Chase Stinsen track the legendary Golden Trinity, they must learn to put their differences aside and depend on one another to survive. (978-1-63555-325-3)

Where We Are by Annie McDonald. A sensual account of two women who discover a way to walk on the same path together with the help of an Indigenous tale, a Canadian art movement, and the mysterious appearance of dimes. (978-1-63555-581-3)